**W9-AUB-832**

In Loving Memory of My Sister,

Jennifer Neri-Lorette
2010/11

Love, Michelle

THE Accidental CHEERLEADER

Wm J Johnston Middle School
360 Norwich Ave.
Colchester, CT 06415

check out these other
candy apple books:

The Boy Next Door
by Laura Dower

Miss Popularity
by Francesco Sedita

How to Be a Girl in Ten Days
by Lisa Papademetriou

THE
accidental
CHEERLEADER

by MIMI McCOY

SCHOLASTIC INC.

New York   Toronto   London   Auckland   Sydney
Mexico City   New Delhi   Hong Kong   Buenos Aires

If you purchased this book without a cover, you should be aware that this book is stolen property. It was reported as "unsold and destroyed" to the publisher, and neither the author nor the publisher has received any payment for this "stripped book."

No part of this publication may be reproduced in whole or in part, stored in a retrieval system, or transmitted in any form or by any means, electronic, mechanical, photocopying, recording, or otherwise, without written permission of the publisher. For information regarding permission, write to Permissions, 557 Broadway, New York, NY 10012.

ISBN-13: 978-0-439-89056-4
ISBN-10: 0-439-89056-X

Copyright © 2006 by Mimi McCoy

All rights reserved. Published by Scholastic Inc., 557 Broadway, New York, NY 10012. SCHOLASTIC, CANDY APPLE, and associated logos are trademarks and/or registered trademarks of Scholastic Inc.

12 11 10 9   9 10 11/0

Printed in the U.S.A.   40

First printing, September 2006

CHAPTER
One

"Check these out!" Kylie Lovett exclaimed.

She yanked the hanger off the rack and held the jeans up to her waist. They were dark indigo with a flare at the ankles. A dragon embroidered in red and gold thread crawled down the left leg.

Her friend Sophie's hazel eyes widened. "Ooh, *serious* shivers," she said. "Shivers" was Sophie and Kylie's word for anything that was so cool it practically sent chills down your spine.

She looked at the price tag. "Make that serious shivers and *on sale*. I swear you have the best shopping karma of anyone I know, Kylie."

Not like me, Sophie thought with a sigh. She found it practically impossible to find stylish clothes that fit her tiny four-foot-nine-inch frame. At twelve years old, she was still the same height she'd been

1

in fifth grade. As far as Sophie was concerned, the Juniors section in the department store might as well have been called Too Big for Sophie Smith.

"Never fear," Kylie told Sophie. She plunged her hands back into the rack and rapidly began to sift through the hangers. A second later, she pulled out an identical pair of jeans in a smaller size.

"Last pair," she declared. "And they look like they might fit you."

Sophie grinned. "You rock, stylie Kylie."

"Anything for my girl."

Draping the jeans over their arms, the two girls made their way toward the fitting rooms. In a week, school would begin, and the store was crowded with kids hitting the back-to-school sales. Sophie glanced around to see if she recognized any faces from Meridian Middle School, but no one looked familiar.

Whenever she thought about school, Sophie felt a little jolt of excitement. This year she and Kylie would be in seventh grade. Sophie thought seventh grade seemed like the perfect age. You were no longer a scared middle-school newbie like the sixth-graders, and you weren't *about* to be a scared high-school newbie like the eighth-graders. You were right in the middle, and Sophie was a right-in-the-middle kind of person.

When they reached the dressing rooms, the bored-looking attendant took the clothes and counted the hangers.

"There's only one room open," she informed them, handing the jeans back. "One of you will have to wait."

Kylie's eyes widened. "Oh, no, ma'am. I'm afraid that's impossible."

The woman folded her arms and raised her eyebrows.

"You've heard of color blindness, right?" Kylie went on, undeterred. "Well, my friend here," she pointed at Sophie, "is pattern blind. She can't tell paisley from stripes. A real fashion disaster." She leaned in closer to the woman and lowered her voice. "For everyone's sake, it's probably better if I go with her."

The attendant frowned. But before she could say anything, Kylie grabbed Sophie's wrist and sashayed past her to the open dressing room.

As soon as they'd shut the door to the tiny cubicle, the friends burst into giggles.

"Pattern blind?" Sophie said.

Kylie shrugged. "It was the first thing I thought of. No offense or anything."

"None taken."

Sophie sat on the bench to untie her sneakers.

Kylie kicked off her flip-flops and yanked the dragon jeans up under her short, flounced skirt. Then she undid the skirt and let it fall around her ankles, all before Sophie had even managed to take off her shoes.

"Judy Lovett's speed shopping rule number one: Wear slip-on shoes for quick changes," Kylie advised. "In the time you spend untying laces you could be scoring a bargain."

Sophie rolled her eyes and yanked off her shoes. Kylie's mom was a real estate agent. She was always zipping around town trying to sell expensive houses to people. She was a pro at shopping on the run. Kylie's mom could find, try on, and purchase an entire outfit in under seven minutes. Sophie had seen her do it. It was pretty impressive, but in her opinion it wasn't a very fun way to shop.

A moment later she'd donned the smaller pair of dragon jeans. The two friends stood squeezed together, side by side in the mirror.

Although their jeans matched, the girls who looked back at them couldn't have been more different. Kylie was five inches taller than Sophie. She had big green eyes, a wide mouth, and golden hair that sprang from her head in tight ringlets. "Striking" was the word Sophie's mom always used to describe Kylie. She wasn't beautiful exactly, but there was

4

something about her face that made you want to keep looking. It always seemed to be on the verge of a hundred different expressions.

Sophie thought her own looks were pretty average. Bobbed brown hair, small nose, freckles. Nothing striking there, Sophie thought, except for her cheeks. They turned raspberry red whenever she felt even a tiny bit embarrassed, which for Sophie was about ten times a day.

Sophie sucked in her cheeks like a super-model and turned sideways to get a better look at the jeans.

"Those jeans fit you perfectly, Soph," Kylie said.

They *did* fit perfectly. The cuffs just covered the tops of her feet, and the legs were fitted but not too snug. The dragon's body ran up the side in a long, undulating wave.

Sophie turned and checked out her other side. Something about the jeans made her look taller, she thought.

"Yours look good, too," she said, checking Kylie in the mirror. Then again, everything looked good on Kylie.

Kylie did a little spin, examining herself from all angles. "Sold!" she declared.

As she changed back into her shorts, Sophie looked again at the price tag on the jeans. Even on sale, they were expensive — almost fifty dollars with tax.

Sophie did the math. For fifty dollars, she could probably buy four T-shirts. Or a sweater and a bunch of socks. Or she could go to the movies eight times and still have money left over for popcorn. Or . . .

"Just get them, Soph," Kylie said suddenly. She was standing over Sophie with her hands on her hips, smirking. "Stop thinking about everything you *should* buy and just get them. They look great on you."

Sophie grinned. She and Kylie had been friends since first grade. They could practically read each other's thoughts. Kylie knew that if Sophie had a dollar in her pocket, she would spend ages trying to decide whether to buy one pack of gum, two candy bars, or ten watermelon chews — and Sophie knew that if Kylie had a dollar in her pocket, she would probably lose it before they even got to the candy store.

But Kylie was right this time, she thought. She had to buy the jeans. They would be the perfect thing to wear on the first day of school.

Sophie giggled. "Come on," she said. "Let's pay for these and go get something to eat. I'm starving."

At the register, Sophie pulled out her credit card and handed it to the cashier. She felt a twinge of pride remembering the day a few months before when her parents had given her the card. "You're old enough now to be responsible," her dad had said, solemnly placing it in her hands. Sophie's parents weren't rich, and she knew her father especially worried about money, so it made her that much prouder to know that they trusted her.

As Sophie signed the credit card receipt, Kylie spun a display rack of jewelry around. "Ooh!" she said, stopping at a pair of dangly earrings. "Shiverlicious!"

She took the earrings off the rack and set them on the counter next to her jeans. A moment later, she added a bracelet. Then she took a tiny bottle of glittery nail polish from a nearby display and added that to the pile, too.

The young woman behind the counter rang up Kylie's purchases.

"Hmm," said Kylie when she saw the total. She pulled some bills out of her wallet and counted them. She counted them again. She searched around in the bottom of her purse.

The cashier tapped her long orange fingernails against the register, waiting.

Kylie picked up the earrings, bracelet, and nail polish. "I'm just going to put these back," she told the cashier.

The woman sighed and retotaled Kylie's bill.

The minute she had heard that Sophie had a credit card, Kylie had rushed to her parents and asked for one, too. They said no before she'd even finished her sentence. They knew better. Kylie was very impulsive — when she saw something she liked, she bought it. She could max out a credit card in a single trip to the mall.

As they exited the store, Sophie swung her shopping bag and did a happy little skip. "Total score!" she exclaimed. "We are going to look so great on the first day of school."

"Absolutely," Kylie agreed. Then she frowned. "But we can't *both* wear them on the first day."

Sophie stopped swinging the bag. "Why not?"

"'Cause it's not *cool*. We can't be all matchy-matchy on the first day of seventh grade. Everyone would think that we're big losers who have to do everything together."

"Oh." Sophie hadn't thought of that. In sixth grade, she had seen lots of friends wearing the same necklaces or jackets or sneakers. And besides, she and Kylie *did* do everything together.

But maybe Kylie knew something about seventh grade that she didn't.

"And since we can't both wear them on the first day," Kylie went on, thinking aloud, "I guess it's only fair that neither of us do."

"I guess." Sophie wondered what she would wear instead. The whole point of this shopping trip had been to find her first-day outfit.

They had almost reached the food court. Sophie could smell french fries and cinnamon buns. She started to head toward a pretzel stand, but Kylie grabbed her arm.

"Can we go into the Cut Above?" she asked, pointing to the store across from them. "Just for a second?"

Sophie shrugged. "Sure." The Cut Above sold crazy, expensive gadgets, like chairs that massaged you while you were sitting in them and alarm clocks that woke you up with recordings of real bird sounds. She wondered why Kylie wanted to go there. But before she could ask, Kylie had turned and was making a beeline into the store. Sophie hurried after her.

"Look at this," Sophie said when they were inside. She picked up a robotic dog. "'The perfect pet,'" she read from the box. "'Never needs to be fed or walked. Odor-free. Hair-free. Noise-free.' How about fun-free? What do you think, Kye? Should we get it for your mom?"

Kylie didn't answer. She was staring at something across the room.

Sophie followed her gaze. Three boys from Meridian were gathered around a plasma TV against the opposite wall, playing a simulated golf game. The tall one, Scott Hersh, was the football team's star quarterback. The other two guys, Jake and Dominick, were his best buds. They would all be eighth-graders this year.

Now Sophie understood why she and Kylie were there. Kylie had a crush on Scott. Half the girls at Meridian did. Last year Scott had won the district all-star award for football, and he was part of the most popular clique at school.

As Kylie stared, Scott glanced in their direction. Quickly, Kylie pretended to be examining the display in front of her. It was a table of electric nose-hair clippers.

"I don't know if I'd get those if I were you," Sophie said, sidling over to her. "I hear Scott Hersh likes girls with really long nose hair."

Kylie smiled sheepishly. She set down the nose-hair clippers and moved over to the next display. KARAOKE IN YOUR OWN HOME! the sign read.

"I love karaoke!" said Kylie.

She began to fiddle with the dials on the machine. A second later, the opening phrase of a pop song burst from the speaker. Kylie picked up the mic and started to sing.

Heat rushed to Sophie's cheeks as if someone had lit a match underneath them. Why did Kylie have to live out her pop idol fantasies right now, she wondered, when three of the most popular guys at Meridian were playing simulated sports just twenty feet away?

A few people in the store turned to look. Sophie glanced over at the boys, but they were still absorbed in their game.

Kylie's eyes were shut tight and she had her head thrown back, singing like a true pop diva. Sophie sighed. She loved her friend's outgoingness, but sometimes she wished she didn't have to be so . . . well, *outgoing*. Hanging out with Kylie could be sort of like riding a roller coaster. Ninety-nine percent of the time it was a blast, but every now and then she did something that made you want to scream.

Out of the corner of her eye, Sophie saw Scott and his friends turn around.

They're coming over here! she thought. *What should I do?*

11

For a brief instant she considered unplugging the karaoke machine. Then she realized that, without music, Kylie would just keep singing, which would be even more embarrassing.

Stop freaking, Sophie told herself. *Just calm down.* After all, she didn't even know these guys. Who cared what they thought?

But the truth was, Sophie cared. She didn't like to attract attention, good or bad. She might not be the most popular girl at school, but she wasn't the biggest geek, either. She thought of herself as a nice, normal person, and she thought other people probably saw her that way, too. At least, she hoped they did.

In Sophie's opinion, an impromptu pop concert at a high-end home electronics store did not make her seem like a nice, normal person. Kylie might as well have hung a flashing sign over their heads, LOOK AT US! in neon lights.

Sophie closed her eyes and willed the moment to be over as soon as possible.

A second later, it was. As she opened her eyes, she was just in time to see the boys' backs as they headed out the door of the store.

CHAPTER
Two

Sophie leaned against her locker and checked her watch for the third time that morning. Eight-fifteen. Kylie was late.

The hall was starting to fill with students. Noise echoed through the corridor as they hollered greetings, excited to see one another after the summer. A few kids Sophie knew said hi as they passed her. They all were wearing bright clothes in the latest fashions. They sported new haircuts and dark tans, and the ones who'd gotten their braces off flashed extra-wide pearly white smiles.

The first day of the school year wasn't really like school at all, Sophie thought. It was more like a commercial for school. All the kids wore cool clothes and looked happy, the teachers acted nice, and the classes actually seemed interesting. It was like watching a movie preview that turns out to be way better than the movie itself.

As she waited for Kylie, Sophie eyed her own lime green corduroys. She wished she'd worn something else. The pants were too heavy for the warm late-summer morning. But she'd promised Kylie she wouldn't wear the dragon jeans, and these were her only other new pants.

"Sophie!"

Kylie rushed up, her blond curls bouncing like hair in a shampoo commercial. She threw her arms around Sophie as if they hadn't seen each other in years, even though they'd talked on the phone just the night before.

"Sorry I'm late," Kylie said breathlessly. "I missed the bus, so my mom had to drive, but she couldn't find the car keys. Boy, was she mad —"

She broke off when she saw Sophie staring at her. "What?" Kylie asked.

"Your jeans," Sophie said.

"What?" Kylie looked at her legs. "Did I spill something on them? What is it? Toothpaste?" She craned her neck, looking for stains.

"You wore *the* jeans," Sophie said, eyeing the red-and-gold dragon on Kylie's left leg. "Kye, we agreed that *neither* of us would wear those on the first day of school. Remember?"

14

Kylie's eyes opened so wide Sophie could see white all around her irises. "Ooooops! I totally forgot, Soph. I was running late, and my mom was yelling at me to hurry. So I grabbed the first thing —"

"Whatever. Forget it," Sophie said, cutting her off. *It's just like Kylie to forget her own rule,* she thought.

"Really, Soph, I forgot. You aren't mad, are you? They're just jeans."

"Right," said Sophie.

The thing was, Sophie knew Kylie hadn't meant to break her rule. She sometimes did things without thinking. Sophie knew that. She was used to it.

So why did she feel so annoyed?

She tried to shrug off the feeling. Sophie didn't like to make a big deal out of things. "So, what do you think of my locker?" she asked, changing the subject.

Her locker was in the sunny southeast corridor on the second floor. Normally, seventh-graders were assigned lockers on the lower floors. But this year their class was bigger than usual, so some of them had been given lockers in the upstairs hallways, near the eighth-graders.

"You're lucky you got a good one," said Kylie. "Mine's across from the cafeteria. The whole hallway smells like barfburgers." Barfburgers was what Kylie called school food, whether it was a burger or not. She claimed it was all made from the same mystery substance, and it all made you want to barf.

"Yeah, it's nice up here," Sophie agreed, looking around.

Kylie suddenly gasped. "And I just saw something that makes it a whole lot nicer! Scott sighting, dead ahead."

Sophie turned. Across the hallway, Scott Hersh was leaning casually against a row of lockers, talking to a friend. As they watched, he turned and put his bag inside the locker directly across from Sophie's.

"I cannot believe your locker is right across from Scott Hersh's!" Kylie's whisper was so loud, Sophie was sure Scott could hear it on the other side of the hallway. "You are the luckiest girl alive."

"I guess."

Sophie didn't get why everyone was so into Scott. He was good-looking, she supposed. He had deep brown eyes and a scar above his lip that gave him a cute, crooked smile. But Sophie thought he seemed aloof and unfriendly. He didn't talk much,

16

and when he did it was only with other football players.

"Trade lockers with me," Kylie pleaded.

"Nope," said Sophie.

"I'll be your best friend."

It was an old joke between them. They had already been best friends for almost as long as either of them could remember. "You wouldn't send your best friend down to barfburger hall, would you?" asked Sophie.

Kylie sighed. "You're right. I could never do that to you. I guess it just means I'm going to be here *all the time*."

"Fine with me."

Just then, there was a ripple in the flow of hallway movement. Several kids turned to look as a quartet of girls strode down the center of the corridor.

In the lead was a petite girl with almond-shaped eyes and long wavy black hair that reached halfway down her back. Everyone in school knew Keisha Reyes. She was head of the cheerleading team and the most popular girl at Meridian. The red-haired girl to her right, walking so close that she matched Keisha's steps, was her best friend, Courtney Knox. Following on their heels were two blonde girls — Amie and Marie Gildencrest, the only identical twins at Meridian Middle School. Courtney, Amie, and Marie were all cheerleaders, too.

As they walked down the hall, the girls shouted greetings to the other popular eighth-graders. Keisha had a perfect smile, Sophie noticed. It was wide and full of even, white teeth. Courtney, on the other hand, looked like she was pouting even when she wasn't. Sophie thought it was because of all the lip gloss she wore.

"Heeeey, Scott!" Keisha called flirtatiously as she passed.

Scott flashed his crooked grin and waved at her.

Someone called Sophie's and Kylie's names. A boy's voice. Confused, Sophie pulled her gaze from the cheerleaders and looked around. There was Joel Leo making his way toward them through the crowded hallway.

Joel had moved in down the street from Kylie the year before, at the beginning of sixth grade. They had become friends riding the bus together. Sophie had gotten to know him a little, too, when she took the bus home with Kylie after school.

"Joel-e-o!" Kylie exclaimed.

"Hey, Joel," said Sophie.

"What's up, guys?" he said. "How was your summer?"

"Oh, you know, the usual," Kylie answered, with a bored wave of her hand. "Jetting to Hollywood. Shopping in London. Sunbathing in Saint Trapeze."

Joel smiled. "You mean Saint-Tropez?"

"Yeah, there, too," Kylie said.

Joel and Sophie laughed. "We mostly hung out at the pool," Sophie told him. "What about you?"

"Yeah, I didn't see you around," Kylie added.

"I was in California helping out on my aunt and uncle's farm," Joel told them. "They grow organic kiwis. Weird, huh?"

"Weird," Sophie agreed. "But it sounds kind of cool, too."

"It was pretty cool. They paid me six dollars an hour to pick fruit, and I got to eat all the kiwis I wanted. I don't really like them, though. Kiwis, I mean. They're all furry."

"Gross!" Kylie said. "So you spent the summer eating furry fruit? Sounds like a blast."

Joel smiled. "Naw, most of my family lives around there, too. I have some cousins who are pretty cool. They taught me how to surf."

The way he said "surf" gave Sophie a little chill. She tried to imagine Joel eating tropical fruit and surfing in southern California. It seemed incredibly exotic compared to hanging out by the pool. Sophie

19

always found Joel slightly mysterious. He didn't look like most of the other boys at Meridian. His hair was long and a little shaggy, and he wore T-shirts for bands that Sophie had never heard of. Even his name was unusual. Joel Leo. If you took off the *J* it was the same spelled forward and backward.

What impressed Sophie most, though, was how laid-back Joel seemed. She couldn't imagine starting middle school in a new town where you didn't know anyone, but Joel didn't seem to mind at all. In sixth grade, he'd been just as friendly with the math nerds as he was with the skaters and the soccer players. As far as Sophie could tell, he wasn't part of any clique. He got along with a lot of different kids.

Sophie noticed how his teeth stood out white against his brown face. *He got tan over the summer,* she thought. *He looks good. In fact, he's cute. Way cute.*

As quickly as the thought came, Sophie pushed it away. Kylie and Joel were neighbors, and their parents were friends. She knew their families sometimes had dinner together, which in Sophie's mind practically made them related. If Kylie found out she had a crush on Joel, she'd never hear the end of it.

The bell for first period rang loudly, startling Sophie out of her thoughts.

"Well, I better go," Joel said. "I'll see you guys later." His eyes rested on Sophie for a moment. She felt the beginnings of a blush creep into her cheeks.

"Later, Joeleo," Kylie said cheerfully.

"Bye," Sophie murmured.

"Hey, by the way, Kylie," Joel said as he walked away, "cool pants!"

Kylie beamed. Sophie gritted her teeth, hating her lime green cords.

Later that day, Sophie stretched her legs across the seat in the last row of the bus. She worked the flavor out of a piece of cinnamon gum.

Kylie was sprawled out on the seat in front of Sophie, and Joel lounged in the seat across the aisle. Sophie was going over to Kylie's as she usually did after school, and both Kylie's and Joel's houses were the last stop on the bus route. The bus was mostly empty now, so they had taken over the back rows of seats.

"I heard Keisha was dating a high-school guy over the summer," Kylie reported.

Kylie had spent the last fifteen minutes reviewing the summer gossip she'd picked up at school. Most of it centered around Keisha Reyes.

"I heard she dumped him right before school started," Kylie went on. "And he spent every night for a week calling her on the phone, crying and begging her to get back together. Can you imagine? A high-school guy!"

"What grade in high-school?" Joel asked.

"I'm not sure. Ninth, I think."

"Big deal. If he's in ninth grade that means he was in eighth grade last year. Which means he's practically the same age as Keisha," Joel pointed out.

Kylie shrugged defensively. "It's just what I heard."

"Anyway, I'm tired of hearing about Keisha Reyes. She's a snob," said Joel.

"Maybe people just *think* she's a snob because she's a cheerleader and she's pretty and popular. Maybe she's actually really nice. She has nice hair," Kylie pointed out.

"That's great logic, Kylie," Joel said. "Just because someone has nice hair doesn't mean she's a nice person."

Sophie sighed and let her attention drift. She wondered what it would be like to have a guy beg you to get back together. The crying part sounded awful, she decided. But it still would be nice to have a guy like you so much he called every night.

Sophie had never had a boyfriend. Not a real one, anyway. In fourth grade a boy named Tyler had asked her to go out with him, but they didn't go anywhere and it didn't really mean anything. But she knew having a boyfriend was different in middle school. Girls held their boyfriends' hands. They hung out by their lockers and went to the movies. They even kissed.

She glanced across the aisle at Joel. He was wearing a black T-shirt that said THE RAMONES in bold white letters. A loop of his long light brown hair fell against his cheek. He tucked it behind his ear. Unconsciously, Sophie brought her hand to her face and tucked her own hair behind her ear.

Joel felt her gaze and looked over. When he met Sophie's eyes, he smiled. Quickly, Sophie turned her attention back to Kylie.

"Anyway," Kylie was saying, "I guess we'll know what they're all like pretty soon. We're probably going to be spending a lot of time with them."

"Spending a lot of time with whom?" Sophie asked. "What are you talking about?"

"Keisha and the other cheerleaders," Kylie told her. "Tryouts for the team are next week. I think we have a shot at making it."

"You're trying out for cheerleading?" Sophie was surprised. Kylie hadn't mentioned it before.

Kylie's smile could have lit up a football stadium. "Nope. *We're* trying out. I signed you up, too!"

There was a squeal of brakes as the bus lurched to a halt at Joel and Kylie's stop. Sophie sat bolt upright and stared over the seat back at her friend. "You did *what*?"

CHAPTER
Three

"No. No way. Absolutely not." Sophie squeezed her eyes shut and shook her head from side to side as if trying to erase the idea from the air with her nose.

For the last twenty minutes, Kylie had been telling her how great cheerleading would be. But Sophie wasn't buying it.

"Come on, Soph. It will be fun," Kylie pleaded.

"Fun? Yeah, the way total humiliation is fun," Sophie fumed.

Sophie, Kylie, and Joel were sitting on the deck in Kylie's backyard. A bag of potato chips, a two-liter bottle of soda, and a pack of cherry-flavored licorice whips sat open on the patio table in front of them. Sophie's parents hardly ever bought junk food, and normally she loved eating at Kylie's. But right now she was too angry to be hungry.

"I cannot believe you signed me up for cheerleading tryouts without even asking me, Kye. Do I *look* like a cheerleader? I mean, I can't even talk in class without blushing." She glanced at Joel and, as if to prove her point, turned beet red.

Joel didn't seem to notice. "But you used to go to gymnastics meets, right?" he asked casually, reaching into the bag and scooping up a handful of chips.

Sophie had taken gymnastics lessons, all through grade school. She'd won all-around second place in the last citywide meet she went to, just before she quit.

She shrugged. "Yeah. So?"

"So didn't you have to compete in front of lots of people then?"

"That was different," said Sophie, willing her cheeks to return to their normal color. "All that mattered was whether I landed a back handspring or not. I was being judged on my skills, not my hair or clothes or how cool I was."

"It isn't all that different," argued Kylie. "And anyway, you won't be in front of the entire school. The only people who see the tryouts are the coach and the eighth-grade cheerleaders."

"Oh, *only* the eighth-grade cheerleaders. *Only*

the most popular girls in school." Sophie rolled her eyes. "No way, José. Do it without me."

"I *can't* do it without you. You have to try out with a partner. That's the rule."

Sophie located a stray chip on the table. She stabbed it with her thumb, breaking it into pieces. "So find another partner."

With a little huff, Kylie sat back in her chair. "If I'd known you would freak out like this I would have."

Sophie said nothing. She continued to pulverize the potato chip.

Kylie tried a different tack. "Soph, remember last year, when we did the school play?"

The year before, Kylie had gotten a small role in the school play, and she'd convinced Sophie to do backstage crew. It had been Sophie's job to make sure all the actors were in their places and to pull the rope that opened the stage curtains. She remembered the tingly feeling of excitement she'd had standing in the wings with everyone just before they went on.

In fact, most of the exciting things Sophie had ever done had been Kylie's idea. When Kylie ran for class president in fifth grade, she'd made Sophie her campaign manager. It had even been Kylie's

27

idea, back in first grade, to take gymnastics classes together. Kylie had quit after only a month, bored by the endless exercises. It was Sophie who'd gone on to become a gymnast.

But all that was different, Sophie reminded herself. Controlling the curtains backstage was not the same as cheerleading.

"Sophie, I could never have gone onstage every night if I hadn't known you were there watching," Kylie told her now. "And I can't imagine doing this without you, either. It just wouldn't be as fun. So, will you do it? Please? I'll be your best friend."

Sophie swept the chip crumbs off the table and into her open palm. Then she leaned over the edge of the deck and tossed them onto the grass. She thought about how she always went along with Kylie's ideas.

Kylie watched her, waiting for an answer.

"No," Sophie said at last.

Kylie's face tightened. She scraped her chair back and stood up. Without a word, she marched into the house, sliding the screen door shut behind her with a bang. A moment later, Sophie heard the television come on in the Lovetts' living room.

"I think you should do it," Joel said suddenly.

Sophie looked over at him in surprise. "What?"

"I think you should try out."

"Why?" She'd assumed that Joel thought the tryouts were a bad idea, too. "I'd be the worst cheerleader ever. I'd probably make the crowd want to cheer for the other team."

"No, you wouldn't," Joel said. "You'd be good at the cartwheels and handsprings and stuff. Besides, Kylie isn't asking you to be a cheerleader. She just wants you to be her partner for the tryouts."

"But I thought you thought cheerleading was lame. You just said Keisha Reyes is a big snob."

"I said Keisha Reyes is a big snob," Joel replied. "That doesn't necessarily mean I think cheerleading is lame. Look, if you don't make the team, it's no big deal. After a week, no one will even remember that you tried out. And if you do make it, well, you'll be with Kylie, just like she said."

"Kylie only wants to be a cheerleader so she can hang out around Scott Hersh all the time," Sophie blurted.

Joel studied her for a second. "I don't see what's wrong with wanting to hang out with someone you like," he said softly.

Sophie chewed her lip. She felt outnumbered. It was two against one in favor of Sophie Smith trying out for cheerleader. Or make that, cheer*loser*.

"All right," she said with a sigh. "I'll think about it."

"Sophie, you have to *smile!*" Kylie exclaimed. "You look like you're directing air traffic, not rooting for a touchdown."

Sophie stopped midcheer and dropped her arms. "I *was* smiling," she snapped. "Wasn't I?"

"Not unless you call this smiling." Kylie grimaced as if she'd stubbed her toe.

It was Saturday afternoon. The girls were in Kylie's backyard, practicing their routine for the cheerleading tryouts.

Every day after school that week, Sophie and Kylie had gone to training sessions held by the eighth-grade cheerleaders. All the girls who wanted to try out were supposed to pick one cheer and develop a routine with a partner. Tryouts would be the following Monday after school.

With a groan, Sophie flopped down on the grass and covered her face with her arms. "I'm no good at this," she said. "I am going to totally humiliate myself."

"No, you're not," Kylie replied. She marched over, grabbed Sophie's hand, and pulled her back onto her feet. "Now try it again. From the top."

Kylie sat at the edge of the deck, and Sophie stood on the lawn, facing her. "Ready, o-kay!" she shouted.

"We're the Mules, we can't be beat. So clap your hands and stomp your feet. . . ."

She began to go through their routine, lifting her knees, bending her arms into stiff, precise shapes. Sophie actually liked the movements. They reminded her a little of the dance steps in a gymnastics tumbling routine.

"We're the Mules, we make the rules, we trample all those other schools. . . ."

"Bigger smile!" Kylie called out.

It was the smiling that Sophie found hard. She felt like a big dumb Barbie doll with a phony smile plastered across her face.

She stretched her lips wider to show she was trying.

"Now you look like a dog that's about to bite someone," Kylie told her.

Sophie stopped cheering and glared. "I *feel* like I want to bite someone," she said meaningfully.

"Okay." Kylie stood up. "You take a break. I'll practice and you can give me pointers. Be brutal. I can take it."

The girls traded places.

"Ready. O-KAY!" Kylie shouted. She started to move through the cheer.

Watching her, Sophie thought it looked like a completely different routine. Where Sophie tried to be precise and angular, Kylie looked like she was made of rubber. Her kicks wobbled. Her curls bounced. Her arms flapped like wet spaghetti. But Sophie had to hand it to her. Kylie's smile was perfect. From her expression you'd think she'd never had more fun in her life.

By the time she'd finished, Kylie was panting. "What did you think?" she asked between breaths.

"You need to keep your legs straighter on your kicks," Sophie advised. "But otherwise you looked really good."

Kylie plopped down in the grass beside her friend. "I was thinking. We need to have a big ending. Something that will make the judges be all, like, 'Wow!'"

"Like what?" Sophie asked.

"Well, you could do some gymnastics trick," Kylie suggested. "An aerial cartwheel, maybe. Or even a back handspring."

Sophie frowned. "I don't know. They didn't say anything about tumbling at the practices. It seems kind of show-offy."

Kylie rolled her eyes. "Duh, Sophie. Cheerleading *is* show-offy. That's the point. To show off your cool moves and get the crowd psyched."

"Well . . ." Sophie plucked a handful of grass from the lawn. "What would you do?"

"I could do a cartwheel or something. If we're both doing it at the same time, it won't really matter."

"Can you even *do* a cartwheel?" asked Sophie.

"Sure."

"Show me."

Kylie got up from the lawn. Raising her arms over her head, she took a step as if she was about to cartwheel. But at the last second she pulled back. She took another step and faltered again.

"On the count of three," said Sophie. "One, two, *three!*"

Kylie placed both hands on the ground and kicked her legs in the air.

She looks like a donkey trying to buck something off its back, Sophie thought. *Or a cat falling headfirst out of a tree.* One thing was certain, it was no cartwheel.

Kylie righted herself. "I know. Not perfect. But you can coach me, right?"

Sophie sighed. It wouldn't be easy to teach Kylie how to do a cartwheel in a day and a half. But she could see that her friend had made up her mind.

And if they were going to do stunts at the

end of their routine, Sophie thought, they ought to look good. Better than good. They ought to look perfect.

She stood and brushed off the back of her shorts. "Okay," she said, positioning herself next to Kylie. "This is how you start."

CHAPTER
Four

Monday morning, Sophie woke with a feeling of doom.

It stayed with her while she showered and dressed. At breakfast, it turned her cornflakes to glue in her mouth. It made her forget to bring her book to Spanish class, and in social studies, it even made her forget her own last name. She had to think for a minute before she wrote it at the top of her paper.

By the time she and Kylie made their way to the gym after school, the feeling was so strong Sophie was certain it was visible — an ugly gray cloud clinging to her like fog.

"I'm so nervous!" Kylie whispered as they walked through the gym doors.

Sophie nodded. "Nervous" didn't even begin to

cover it. She felt like she was about to walk the plank.

Any minute now, the cheerleading tryouts would begin. Sophie, Kylie, and a group of other seventh-grade girls stood at the back of the gym, waiting for the coach to arrive.

From where she was standing, Sophie could see patches of blue sky out the high gym windows. The weather had finally cooled into the kind of clear September day that normally made her want to spread her arms wide and shout for joy. At that moment she would have given anything to be outside.

She would have given anything to be anywhere but here.

In the center of the gym, the six eighth-grade cheerleaders were sitting at a table that had been set up on the half-court line. Courtney, lip-glossed and perfectly coiffed, as usual. The twins, whose blond hair was braided into identical pigtails. At the end of the table sat the two other girls, named Alyssa Craig and Renee Ramirez. Alyssa was pretty, with arched eyebrows and black hair that curled up at the ends in a smooth flip. Renee was very fair with dark hair she usually wore pulled back in a ponytail. And of course, there was Keisha Reyes, right in the center where she always was.

They were the most popular girls, the royalty of the school. And any minute now they were going to give their undivided attention to shy little Sophie Smith.

To distract herself, Sophie started to go over their routine again in her mind. They had spent all day Sunday in Kylie's backyard practicing over and over until Mrs. Lovett claimed their shouting was giving her a headache and drove them over to Sophie's house to practice there instead. When Sophie had gone to bed that night, she could still hear the words of the cheer ringing in her ears.

The trickiest part was the stunt at the end. The way they'd rehearsed it, Sophie did an aerial cartwheel in one direction while Kylie did a regular cartwheel the opposite way so they crossed each other. It had taken half a day of coaching to get Kylie's cartwheel into shape. When she finally nailed it, Sophie couldn't have been prouder than if they'd actually made the team.

Still, all that practicing hadn't made Sophie any more confident. She knew she wasn't cheerleader material. Even her parents didn't think so. At dinner her father gently reminded her, "It's the effort that counts." And when her mother had come to kiss her good night, she'd told Sophie how proud she was already. Sophie knew that was all code for "We still love you even if you don't make the team."

Sophie closed her eyes. She hid her hands behind her back so no one would see her cross her fingers as she made a wish.

Please, please, please, don't let me make a fool of myself, she pleaded.

She jumped as the door to the gym banged open. A short blond woman walked briskly into the room. She wore a yellow T-shirt that said CHEER ALL OUT OR DON'T CHEER AT ALL. Two other women followed her in.

The blond woman clapped her hands for attention, which wasn't necessary. All talk had stopped the moment she entered the room.

"Okay, ladies!" Her voice seemed to reverberate through the entire gym. Sophie was surprised that such a loud voice could come from such a tiny person.

"I'm Madeline Charge, the adviser for the Meridian Middle School cheerleading squad. If any of you have older sisters, you may already have heard of me. I've been coaching this team for more than ten years, and I like to say that every year our cheerleaders get better."

She flashed a brilliant white smile around the room.

Sophie stared. She had never seen an adult who seemed as perky as Madeline Charge. She just *looked* like a cheerleader, right down to the pink polish on her perfectly painted fingernails.

"Before we begin, I want to introduce you to our two guest judges," Ms. Charge boomed. "This is Ms. Biers. She coaches the Meridian High School cheerleading team." She gestured at the blond woman, who nodded. "And this is Ms. Lytle, captain of the Meridian Community College cheerleaders." Ms. Lytle raised her hand and waved. "Please give them a round of applause. We're very lucky to have them with us today."

The seventh- and eighth-graders dutifully clapped. Ms. Biers and Ms. Lytle beamed like contestants in a beauty pageant. They were very good at smiling, Sophie noticed.

"And of course," Ms. Charge went on, "you already know our other judges, the eighth-grade cheerleaders."

The girls smiled smugly from their chairs.

"So, let me tell you all how this is going to work," said Ms. Charge. She held up a worn-looking baseball cap and explained that each of the teams would draw a number from the hat. That would be the order in which they went. "Got it?" she bellowed.

Around the room, girls nodded.

"Let me just remind you of the rules. When it's your turn to go, take the floor with your partner, say your names, and then start your routine. Your routine shouldn't be longer than one cheer. And no props, including boom boxes. I want to hear you girls shout. Got it?"

They had it. The girls started to shuffle around, straightening their shorts, tying their sneakers, combing their fingers through their hair.

"I'm not through yet, ladies," Ms. Charge boomed. The shuffling stopped. "We have twenty-eight girls trying out," she told them. "There are six open spots on the team. You might end up on the team and your friend might not, or vice versa. I asked you to try out in pairs today because cheer-leading is all about teamwork. And teamwork means that you respect your teammates whether they win or lose. I don't want to hear about sore losers or sore winners. Got it?"

There were a few tentative nods.

It was just like adults to stand around giving lectures about teamwork when all the kids wanted to do was get on with the game, Sophie thought. She rolled her eyes at Kylie to say, "Do you believe this garbage?" But Kylie wasn't looking. Her eyes were glued on Madeline Charge like she was the greatest thing since sliced bologna.

"All right," Ms. Charge said, clapping her hands again. "Let's do this!"

She held up the hat. Several girls hurried over to pick numbers.

Kylie nudged Sophie. "Go ahead, you get it," she whispered.

Sophie was glad to move. Her legs felt stiff from standing in one place for so long. She walked over to Ms. Charge and fished a slip of paper out of the beat-up old hat. On it was written the number four.

Four? Four was too soon. Four meant there were only three pairs of girls ahead of them. Sophie's heartbeat quickened. She took a few shallow breaths.

As Sophie turned to bring the slip back to Kylie, she tripped. Her arms flew out and she barely managed to catch herself before sprawling face-first on the floor. Several people turned to look, including Ms. Charge.

Ms. Charge raised her eyebrows and waggled a finger at Sophie's sneakers. Looking down, Sophie saw that one of her shoelaces was untied.

Cheeks burning, she knelt to tie her shoe. *Perfect,* she thought, *now everyone thinks I'm a klutz and a slob.* Again she wished she were anywhere but here.

Sophie stomped back over to Kylie and handed her the slip of paper.

"Great! Four is perfect!" Kylie said brightly. She didn't mention that Sophie had just made a total fool of herself.

Sophie stared at her friend. What had happened to Kylie all of a sudden? How could she act like everything was great and perfect when everything clearly was awful? She was already acting like a cheerleader, and they hadn't even gotten through tryouts yet!

The judges took their seats in the folding chairs behind the table. Keisha passed out clipboards and little pencils.

"How do I look?" Kylie asked Sophie. She was wearing white shorts, a pink T-shirt, and tennis socks with matching pink pom-poms at the heels. She'd parted her blond curls into two springy pigtails that flopped alongside her head like the ears of a cocker spaniel. They looked goofy but cute, Sophie thought.

"Good. Cheerleaderish," Sophie told her. "How about me?" She'd put on a yellow T-shirt and purple track pants. They were supposed to represent purple and gold, the school colors, though the violet of her pants was too dark and her yellow shirt wasn't quite yellow enough.

"Great," Kylie said. "You look great."

"Okay, pair number one, you're up," Ms. Charge bellowed.

Pair number one turned out to be two girls named Trisha and Kate. Sophie knew them. Everyone did. From the first day of middle school, they'd established themselves as the most popular girls in the class. Sophie wasn't even sure how. They just had it — whatever "it" was.

"Dang," Kylie whispered, eyeing Trisha and Kate's identical purple polo shirts. "We should've worn matching outfits. I didn't think of that."

"Ready, let's go!" Kate and Trisha hollered in unison. They started into their cheer. Their moves were tight and their smiles pert. Their claps made crisp popping sounds.

Sophie glanced over at the judges. Keisha and Courtney were smiling as if they were watching their own little sisters. She knew then that Trisha and Kate were in.

When they were finished, Ms. Charge smiled. "Thank you," she said. She wrote something down on her clipboard. Sophie noticed the other judges writing, too.

Next up were two girls who were pretty and well liked. One of the girls had straight blond hair that she'd pulled into a high ponytail. Sophie thought

43

she looked like a younger version of Madeline Charge.

When they were done, Madeline smiled and thanked them, just as she had Trisha and Kate.

"Pair three," she said when she finished writing on her clipboard.

For a second, no one stepped forward. The girls who were waiting their turn began to look around. Had a group forgotten their number?

Suddenly, there was a flurry of movement. Two girls burst from the sidelines, doing round-offs and back handsprings. When they reached the center of the floor they stopped.

"Amy Martin!" one shouted, standing like a soldier at attention.

"Angie Biggs!" the other shouted.

"Ready, O-KAY!" they cried in unison.

Sophie recognized Amy and Angie, but she never knew which was which. Though one had brown hair and the other was blond, they were both blandly cheerful in a way that made it impossible to tell them apart. Sophie had never paid much attention to them before. But now she couldn't tear her eyes away from them.

They must've been practicing for weeks! she thought. Their movements were perfectly in sync.

Their voices seemed to meld into a single, unified shout.

As they reached the end of their routine, Amy sprang into the air, flipping backward in a standing back tuck, while Angie spotted her. When Amy landed, both girls slid into splits, their arms raised over their heads.

The eighth-grade cheerleaders clapped and whistled. The seventh-graders stared with expressions of dismay. Sophie knew how they felt. How could any of them hope to make the team when this was what they were up against?

Madeline Charge looked like she'd just won the lottery. "*Thank you,* ladies," she said, beaming. "That was very good."

She made a note on her clipboard. Sophie imagined her drawing a big star next to Amy's and Angie's names.

"Okay. Group four, you're up," the coach said.

For a second, Sophie thought she wouldn't be able to move. She felt as if someone had injected ice-cold water into her arms and legs. Then Kylie gave her a little nudge, and before she knew it, she was out on the floor.

"Kylie Lovett!" bellowed Kylie in a good imitation of Ms. Charge.

"Sophie Smith," squeaked Sophie. Her mouth felt as dry as the Sahara.

Ms. Charge looked up from her clipboard. "Volume!" she commanded.

Sophie blushed. "Sophie Smith," she managed in a slightly louder voice. She took a deep breath.

"Ready, O-KAY!" Sophie and Kylie said together.

They had practiced their cheer so many times over the weekend that Sophie could have done it in her sleep. Instead, she concentrated on smiling. She grinned so hard her cheeks started to cramp.

In what felt like seconds, the cheer was over and they had come to the tumbling finale. Sophie was upside down in midair when she realized that Kylie wasn't cartwheeling alongside her. Righting herself, she saw that Kylie was frozen, her arms in the air and her eyes wide.

Oh no! Sophie thought. *She's chickening out!*

To stall for time, Sophie did another aerial cartwheel. To her relief, Kylie started to move. But she didn't cartwheel. Instead, she put her hands on the ground and did a big, clumsy somersault, the kind a toddler would do, straight toward the judges.

Kylie came out of the roll with a giant grin on her face. Behind her, Sophie dropped to one knee.

"Goooooo, Mules!" they shouted.

46

Sophie quickly got to her feet and hurried over to the sidelines. Kylie was right behind her.

"Wasn't that great?" said Kylie, her eyes shining.

Sophie didn't think so. The eight-grade cheerleaders were laughing, and so were some of the seventh-graders. She looked over at the judges. The three women had their heads together, talking.

They hadn't talked after any of the other pairs. Not even after Amy and Angie. What were they saying? Had Sophie and Kylie been *that* bad?

Just then, Ms. Charge glanced over at them. When she saw Sophie looking at her, she smiled.

Sophie felt sick to her stomach. The judges were laughing at them, too. Now she was sure of it.

When Sophie got to her locker Tuesday morning, Kylie was waiting for her.

"They've posted the results," she told Sophie. "The list is right outside the counselor's office. The anticipation is *killing* me."

"You could've looked without me," Sophie pointed out. She wasn't in any hurry to see who'd made the team. It still made her cringe to think about the tryouts the day before.

"I'm too nervous. We have to go together. Come on." Kylie grabbed Sophie's arm.

Sophie let herself be dragged down the hall, still wearing her backpack. Kylie hadn't even given her a chance to drop off her things in her locker.

By the time they got to the counselor's office, the crowd around the posted sheet was three girls deep. Sophie would've preferred to wait her turn, but Kylie was already shouldering her way through. Sophie reluctantly followed in her wake.

The list was printed on yellow paper. Sophie felt her heartbeat quicken as she began to run her eyes down the names.

Then her heart almost stopped. There, right at the end of the list, it said SOPHIE SMITH.

She read her name over and over again, hardly believing her eyes. Then, slowly, her disbelief gave way to another feeling. *I made it,* she thought. *I made it! I got picked over all those other girls. Kylie and I are going to be cheerleaders!*

She turned to Kylie, ready to celebrate. But the look on Kylie's face stopped her.

Kylie was frowning.

Sophie turned back to the list. She'd seen Kylie's name, hadn't she? Yes, there it was, at the very bottom of the page.

"Oh!" Sophie said with a little gasp.

The list read KYLIE LOVETT — MASCOT.

CHAPTER
Five

"A *mule!*" Kylie moaned.

Sophie, Kylie, and Joel were sitting at one of the outdoor tables in the school quad, eating lunch. Kylie had just finished filling Joel in on the results of the tryouts.

"I mean, do I *seem* like I'd be a good mule?"

Sophie hesitated, thinking of the donkeylike kick Kylie had done in her backyard the day before the cheerleading tryouts. Kylie gave her a wounded look.

"No," Sophie said quickly. "You're nothing like a mule."

"There's nothing mulelike about you. Except for your hooves. And your long ears. And your stubborn personality," Joel teased.

Kylie stuck her tongue out at him. "I went to see Ms. Charge after first period," she told them. "And I was, like, 'Why am I the mule?' She said it was because I was funny at the tryouts. They liked my spirit. She acted like that was a good thing."

"Being funny and spirited *are* good things," Joel pointed out.

Kylie sulked. "What a stupid mascot. Why can't it be the Meridian jaguar? Or the Meridian eagle? Or . . . or the Meridian goddess!"

"They don't make goddesses into mascots," Joel told her.

"But it's a good idea, right?" said Kylie. "I mean, I'm not just thinking of me. Having a mule as a mascot makes the whole school look dumb."

"Mules are strong. They're hardworking. They never give up," said Sophie.

"They're also ugly," Kylie grumbled.

"But in a cute way," said Joel.

"Well, maybe you can tell Ms. Charge that you want to be the Meridian goddess this afternoon," said Sophie. "The first practice is right after school."

Kylie plucked two french fries from her lunch tray, swabbed them around in a pool of ketchup, and popped them in her mouth. She chewed for a moment, then pushed her tray away.

"Ugh. I'm not hungry. This whole mule thing has ruined my appetite. Here, you guys have my fries."

Sophie and Joel reached for fries at the same moment, and their fingers touched. Sophie felt an electric sort of tingle her fingertips. Quickly, she pulled her hand away.

"Anyway, I'm not going," said Kylie.

"Not going where?" Sophie asked distractedly. Under the table, her fingers could still feel the brush of Joel's skin. She avoided looking at him.

"To practice. Forget this stuff. I tried out to be a cheerleader, not a mule."

"But" — Sophie was aghast — "but we're supposed to be doing this together! You promised!"

"Well, you don't have to go, either," Kylie pointed out. "You don't even *want* to be a cheerleader. In fact, why don't you quit? Give the spot to someone who really wants it."

"No!" Sophie said, louder than she'd intended. Kylie and Joel both looked at her. She blushed and lowered her voice. "No. We can't just not show up. We tried out and we made it and now we have to do it. That's just how it is." Sophie always followed through on her commitments. She prided herself on it. And she wasn't going to stop now just because Kylie didn't feel like being a mule.

"Fine," said Kylie, a bit huffily. "I'll go to practice. Jeez."

"Give it a chance," Sophie told her, nodding. "That's what I'm going to do. I'm just going to give it a chance."

"STAR. That's a word I want you to remember. You are all Meridian Middle School STARS."

Madeline Charge stood before the cheerleaders, hands on her hips. Today her T-shirt read THERE IS NO "I" IN "TEAM."

The girls sat on the outdoor bleachers, shielding their eyes against the afternoon sunlight. They could hear the boys' football team practicing at the far end of the field. There was an occasional muffled *thud* as the boys banged into one another in their gear.

"Can one of you explain to our new teammates what STAR means?" the cheerleading coach asked, addressing the eighth-graders.

Courtney raised her hand. "Studies. Teamwork. Athleticism. Responsibility," she said primly. She smiled like the teacher's pet.

"Thank you, Courtney. That's right. Studies. Teamwork. Athleticism. Responsibility." Ms. Charge ticked them off one by one on her fingers. "These are the things that you have to focus on to be the best cheerleaders you can be."

Sophie sensed a lecture coming on. She tried to make herself more comfortable on the hard metal seat.

"First of all, *Studies*," Ms. Charge boomed. Even outside, her voice carried. "You all must maintain a C average. We do grade checks once a week. If anyone falls below a C in any class, we have a conference with your teacher. If you don't pull your grade up within a month, you're off the team. Got it?"

The cheerleaders nodded.

"Teamwork." Madeline paced back and forth in front of them like a drill sergeant. "Cheerleading is not about one person being the center of attention. When you're all in a pyramid, the person at the bottom is just as important as the person at the top."

Blah, blah, blah. Sophie hated lectures. She only ever heard them at school, where the adults acted like kids were social morons. Her parents never lectured. If they were disappointed with her, they said, "How do you think you could have done that better?" But they weren't disappointed very often.

Next to Sophie, Kylie snapped her gum. She'd been fidgeting the whole time Ms. Charge was talking. Sophie noticed that Kylie didn't seem to find the coach quite as fascinating as she had at the tryouts.

"Athleticism," the coach went on. "You girls are athletes, and I want you to think of yourselves that way. It's fine to wave pom-poms, but your kicks better be up by your ears or no one cares."

It was true that the girls who had made the team seemed to have been picked more for their athletic skills than their popularity. Trisha and Kate were in, of course, and so were Amy and Angie. But the pretty girl who looked like Ms. Charge hadn't made it, and neither had some other popular girls who'd tried out. The other seventh-grade cheerleader was a girl named Joy. Her eyebrows arched in a way that gave her a constant look of happy surprise, and she had impressed everyone at the tryouts by doing a perfect toe-touch jump.

"Responsibility," Ms. Charge went on in her megaphone voice. "You're expected to show up at practice on time and ready to cheer. If you have to miss a practice, I want to know *before*. Don't come to me with excuses later. I don't want to hear them."

Ms. Charge looked from one face to the next. "You are the STARs of Meridian. But you are all part of the same constellation. One STAR shouldn't outshine the others."

Kylie pretended to stick her finger down her throat. She made a retching noise just loud enough for Sophie to hear.

"Okay. Enough talk," Madeline said, "Now, are you ready to cheer?"

"Yeah!" the other girls cried.

"Uh, Ms. Charge?" Kylie raised her hand. "What should I be doing while everyone else is . . . cheering?"

"Oh, Kylie, our multitalented mascot. You can run drills with the rest of the girls today if you like," said Ms. Charge. "Come see me after practice, and we'll set up a time for you to get your costume."

As the girls got up from the bleachers, Keisha sidled over to Kylie. As usual, Courtney followed at her side.

"I just wanted to say I think you will be a *great* mascot," Keisha told Kylie.

"Really?" Kylie looked pleased.

Keisha nodded. "You were hysterical yesterday at tryouts. It took a lot of nerve. I mean, I could never have gotten up there and embarrassed myself like that in front of a bunch of people. But you made it look totally natural."

Kylie's smile froze. "Thanks," she said uncertainly.

"Anyway, I just wanted to tell you that." With a little smile, Keisha and Courtney walked over to the other cheerleaders to warm up.

Kylie turned to Sophie. "I *embarrassed* myself yesterday?"

"I'm sure that's not what she meant," Sophie said quickly. "She probably just meant that your somersault was original."

Kylie glanced at Keisha's retreating back. "She sure had a nice way of saying it."

The girls spent the next hour doing strengthening exercises. They ran stairs on the bleachers. They did sit-ups and stretches. They worked on their high kicks, cartwheels, and jumps.

By the time they were ready to start learning a cheer, Sophie was sweating. It felt good. She realized how much she'd missed working out since she'd stopped doing gymnastics.

Ms. Charge, who had gone to the equipment room to get the pom-poms, left Keisha in charge of teaching the cheer. As the girls got into rows,

Keisha singled out Kylie. "Not you," she said. "You can't stand in the front row."

"Why not?" asked Kylie.

"Because you're not a cheerleader," said Courtney, coming to stand next to Keisha.

"But if I'm here, I might as well learn the cheer. What if you need a sub or something?" Kylie pointed out.

Keisha wrinkled her nose as if Kylie were something stuck to the bottom of her shoe. "Only the cheerleaders do the cheers. That's why they call them *cheerleaders*."

Kylie pressed her lips together. She didn't move.

Sophie glanced around at the other girls. They were all watching. Alyssa, one of the eighth-graders, had her arms folded and a look of disgust on her face, but Sophie couldn't tell if she was disgusted with Keisha or Kylie.

Keisha gave an exaggerated sigh. "If you really want to learn the cheers, you can stand over there." She pointed to a spot behind the back row.

Kylie looked at Keisha for a second. Then, tossing her curls, she lifted her chin and walked to the spot where Keisha was pointing. Sophie started to follow.

"Not *you*," Keisha said, stopping her. "You have

to stand in front. Otherwise, you won't be able to see anything. You're so small."

Sophie gave Kylie an apologetic look and returned to the front row.

Keisha and Courtney taught a short cheer. Sophie, who was standing between Amy and Angie, was surprised that they already seemed to know it.

"We learned it at cheer camp," Angie explained when Sophie asked.

"You went to cheer camp this summer?" Sophie asked, astonished. In their school district, girls couldn't try out for cheerleading until seventh grade. How could they have gone to camp if they weren't even cheerleaders yet?

"Every summer," Angie told her. "It's not a team cheer camp. It's more like pre-cheer camp for girls who want to be cheerleaders. I've wanted to be a cheerleader since I was five."

"I've wanted to be one since I was four," Amy chimed in from Sophie's right. "My mom was a cheerleader, and my grandma was a cheerleader, too. It's kind of a family tradition."

"Stop talking," Keisha barked. Amy and Angie hushed at once.

Amy and Angie had been going to cheer camp since they were in kindergarten? That explained why their tryout routine had been so good. For the rest of the practice Sophie watched them out of the corner of her eye. There was more to Amy and Angie than she'd thought. Granted, it was a little weird that they'd been practicing to be cheerleaders since before they were even in grade school. But Sophie admired the fact that they were so dedicated.

Finally, Ms. Charge reappeared and announced, "That's it for today. See you all here at the same time tomorrow."

As Sophie and Kylie headed over to the bleachers to collect their things, Kylie said, "Cheerleading is harder than I thought."

Sophie grinned. "Before you know it, you'll be doing back handsprings."

"*If* I come back," Kylie reminded her.

"Kylie!" Ms. Charge walked over to them. "I wanted to find time for you to try on your costume. Can you come by the equipment room next Monday after school?"

Kylie hesitated. At that moment, the boys' football team began to straggle off the field, helmets in their hands, their hair tousled and sweaty. Kylie's gaze landed on one tall figure. Her eyes lit up.

"Sure thing," she said, turning back to Ms. Charge.

"Perfect." Ms. Charge smiled her toothpaste-commercial smile. "See you next week, then."

"Don't we have practice tomorrow?" asked Kylie.

"You don't have to come to all the cheerleading practices," Ms. Charge told her.

"But how will I know the routines?"

"You don't have to know every routine. Mostly what you do is . . . improvise. Run around. Do spirit waves. Make the crowd laugh."

"Make the crowd laugh," Kylie repeated. "Right."

When Ms. Charge was gone, Sophie turned to Kylie. "But if you don't come to practice," she began, "that means . . ."

Sophie looked over at the other cheerleaders with a sinking feeling. *That means I'm on my own.*

CHAPTER
Six

"One, two, hit!"

At the signal, Sophie pushed off Amy's and Angie's shoulders with her hands. Both Amy and Angie were standing in deep lunges. With her right foot braced on Amy's thigh, Sophie lifted her left foot off the ground and brought it up to the top of Angie's thigh. Now she was standing atop their bent legs, balanced between them. Sophie locked her knees and raised her arms in a V.

She held there for one second . . . two seconds . . .

Sophie wobbled. Her foot slipped, and she fell onto the grass.

"Nice try, ladies," barked Ms. Charge. "Angie, your lunge needs to be deeper. I should be able to balance a glass of water on top of your thigh.

Sophie, straight arms! I want to see V for Victory, not U for Unsure. And Alyssa," she turned to Sophie's spotter, who was standing behind Amy and Angie. "Where were you? Let's try it again."

As Amy and Angie set up again, Sophie shook out her legs. After a week of practicing straight cheers, Ms. Charge had started them on stunts, like the thigh stand. Sophie had been surprised by how hard even the easy stunts were. If everyone wasn't doing her part perfectly, the lift didn't work. She was beginning to understand why Ms. Charge was so gung ho about teamwork.

Because she was the smallest person on the team, Sophie had been made a flyer, which meant that she got lifted in the stunts. Keisha and Renee, who were also petite, were the other two flyers. The rest of the girls were bases, who lifted the flyers into the air, or spotters, who helped support them in the lifts and made sure they didn't fall.

"You're doing great," Alyssa told Sophie. She nodded at Renee, who was practicing with another group. "Last year, it took Renee weeks to get this down. You learn fast."

"Thanks," Sophie said, blushing.

"Ready to try again?" asked Alyssa.

Sophie nodded and moved to her spot behind

Amy and Angie. She placed her right foot on Amy's thigh and her hands on both their shoulders.

"One, two, hit!" counted Alyssa.

This time Sophie's foot slid off Angie's thigh before she'd even straightened her legs. Alyssa caught her waist to keep her from falling.

"I think it's time for a break," said Ms. Charge.

Inwardly, Sophie groaned. These were the words she dreaded more than any others, even more than the command "Stairs!" which all the girls hated. She would have happily run fifteen minutes of stairs rather than take a five-minute break with the other cheerleaders.

The girls headed for the bleachers to grab bottles of water and sports drinks.

Sophie pulled a bottle of strawberry-kiwi juice from her backpack and surveyed the scene. Keisha and Courtney were sitting side by side in the grass. Trisha and Kate sat right across from them. Ever since cheerleading practices had started, Keisha, Courtney, Trisha, and Kate had become a tight foursome. In fact, the two popular seventh-graders seemed to have edged out the twins in Keisha's favor. Amie and Marie sat slightly to the side, talking more to each other than anyone else. The other three seventh-graders, Angie, Amy, and Joy, hovered around the edges of the group, drawn like iron filings to a magnet. They were all clearly in awe of Keisha.

Alyssa and Renee also sat at the edge of the group, swigging from Gatorade bottles. Unlike the rest of the cheerleaders they didn't even seem to be trying to be part of Keisha's group. Sophie had noticed they usually sat together during breaks, and she had never once seen them sitting with Keisha's posse at lunch.

During these breaks, Sophie was always in agony over where to sit. No matter where she landed, she felt left out, too shy to chime in on the conversation without feeling stupid. For Sophie, this was the worst part of practice. She wished, not for the first time, that Kylie were here with her.

At last she decided to sit next to Joy. She had just settled on the grass when she heard someone say, "Hey, Itsy-Bitsy."

It took a second before Sophie realized that Keisha was talking to her. Keisha hadn't paid much attention to her, except to give her directions when they were practicing cheers.

"Can I have some of your drink?" she asked Sophie. "I love strawberry-kiwi."

Sophie handed over the bottle at once.

Keisha raised it to her lips, then stopped and

64

gave Sophie a sidelong glance. "You don't have cooties, right?"

Cooties? Sophie thought, baffled. Who talked about cooties in middle school? Still, she didn't want Keisha spreading any rumors that Sophie Smith had cooties. "No," she told her somberly.

Keisha rolled her eyes. "I'm *kidding*."

"Oh."

Keisha took a long drink. When she was done she gave Sophie an appraising look.

"You're pretty," she said. "You have nice eyebrows. But your hair would look better if you parted it on the left side. And you definitely should use mascara. I don't need it. My eyelashes are naturally long and thick, so it would look weird. But yours are really short."

Sophie wasn't sure what to say, so she just nodded.

"I'm going to call you Bitsy," Keisha decided. "For Itsy-Bitsy, because you're so little." When Sophie didn't say anything, she added, "That's better than if I called you Weensy for Teensy-Weensy, right?"

Courtney laughed, and so did Trisha and Kate. Sophie smiled uneasily. She couldn't tell if Keisha was making fun of her or not.

"All right, ladies! Let's get back to work!" Ms. Charge hollered.

"Thanks for the drink, Bitsy. You're sweet." Keisha handed back the bottle of juice. There was only an inch left in the bottom.

Sophie didn't care. Keisha Reyes had told her she had nice eyebrows. *And* she had said she was sweet. *And* she'd given Sophie a nickname! For the first time since Sophie had started cheerleading, she felt sort of like she belonged.

Maybe, she thought, *I'm starting to fit in, after all.*

Friday night, Kylie and Sophie sat curled on the sofa in the Lovetts' living room. Sophie struggled to keep her eyes open as Kylie flipped through the TV channels, looking for something to watch.

Sophie almost always slept over at Kylie's on Fridays. Usually Sophie could stay up all night watching old black-and-white movies. But now it was only ten o'clock, and she was already yawning.

"There's nothing on," Kylie complained. Kylie was a pro channel-changer. She could never settle on one thing. Even if she liked a show, she still had to keep changing channels to see what else was on. If Sophie wanted to watch an entire movie uninterrupted, she usually had to wrestle the remote out of Kylie's hand.

At last, Kylie shut off the TV. "Let's go to my room," she suggested. "We can paint our nails."

On the way to her bedroom, the girls stopped by the kitchen. Kylie took a box of chocolate chip cookies from the cupboard and two cans of soda from the fridge. As an afterthought, she grabbed a bag of pretzels and a jar of peanut butter. Loaded with provisions, they made their way to Kylie's room.

"So," Kylie said, settling herself on the floor. She popped open her soda and twisted the cap off a bottle of purple nail polish. "Tell me how awful cheerleading is."

"It's really not so bad." Sophie picked up a bottle of pink polish and looked at the name on the bottom. Pink Decadence, it was called. "Some of the stunts are hard. But other than that it's okay."

Sophie set down the nail polish and went over to Kylie's mirror. Flipping her hair away from her face, she examined her stubby eyelashes. "Do you have any mascara?" she asked, sifting through the mess of pens, barrettes, tubes of lip gloss, and other junk atop Kylie's dresser.

"No," said Kylie. "Mascara is gross. Your eyelashes are supposed to keep stuff *out* of your eyes. If you put gunk all over them, it kind of defeats the purpose. Anyway, I thought your mom wouldn't let you wear makeup."

"She won't."

Sophie's mom didn't wear any makeup, and she told Sophie she couldn't wear it until she was sixteen. She liked to say, "If you're going to cover your beautiful face with that junk, you'll have to wait until you can drive yourself to the store to buy it."

"I was just curious to see how it would look," Sophie told Kylie. She flipped her hair out of her eyes again.

Kylie glanced up from the toenail she was painting. "What's up with your hair?" she asked.

"It's just something I'm trying."

"Well, you look like a spaz the way you keep jerking your head like that."

"I haven't trained my part yet, that's all," Sophie told her. "So it keeps falling in my eyes."

"Why don't you just use barrettes like you normally do?"

Sophie shrugged. "Barrettes are boring." She was trying to train her hair to part on the left, like Keisha had suggested, but it kept flopping into her eyes. Sophie actually kind of liked it like that. She thought it made her look sophisticated.

"So, tell me about the last practice," Kylie said. "What did Miss Superego do this time?" Kylie came to practice only on Mondays. Most of the practice she sat around waiting for them to finish a cheer so she could jump into the final pose.

Sophie couldn't blame Kylie for hating the practices; she would have been bored just sitting around, too. But it gave Kylie plenty of time to watch the other cheerleaders. She was the one who'd first pointed out to Sophie that Trisha and Kate were in with Keisha, and the twins were out. The way she made it sound, you'd think she spent every Monday afternoon watching some crazy after-school special, and not just the Meridian Middle School cheerleading practice.

"Who are you talking about?" Sophie asked coolly. She knew whom Kylie was talking about, but she didn't feel like going along with her.

"Are you kidding? Keisha, of course. She's got, like, an ego the size of Lake Michigan."

"I guess she can be bossy. But she *is* head cheerleader. It's kind of her job to be bossy."

"Not just bossy. She's sick with power. Joel calls her the Tyrant."

"When were you hanging out with Joel?" Sophie's face felt warm. She hadn't forgotten the tingle she felt when her fingers had brushed Joel's at lunch that day.

Kylie shrugged. "Earlier this week, when you were at practice."

Sophie waited for Kylie to say more. But Kylie was still thinking about the cheerleaders.

"And what about Courtney?" she asked, digging into the box of cookies. "She acts like she's some kind of beauty queen, but she follows Keisha around like a dog on a leash. That's what we can call them. Keisha and Leasha." Kylie laughed.

Sophie frowned. It seemed mean to talk about Courtney behind her back. Courtney had told Sophie she had perfect fingernails. And once she'd loaned Sophie a hair band and hadn't asked for it back. "Ms. Charge says Courtney has the best high kick on the team," she said, feeling she needed to defend her in some way.

"Ms. Charge is a kook," Kylie said through a mouthful of cookies. "'You are all STARs,'" she mimicked. "'But you are all part of the same constellation.' Give me a break."

"Why are you being so negative all of a sudden?" asked Sophie, unable to hide her exasperation. "You were the one who wanted to be a cheerleader in the first place."

"That was before I found out they were all tyrants and followers and kooks."

"Oh? So where do I fall in?"

"Come on, Sophie. I'm not talking about *you*."

"Right."

"Don't freak out. I was just kidding."

Sophie stood up. "I think I'm going to go to bed," she said.

Kylie looked at the clock on her nightstand. "But it's only ten-thirty."

"I'm really tired from practice this week." Sophie crawled into one side of Kylie's double bed and pulled up the covers.

There was a moment of silence.

"You're not much fun tonight," she finally heard Kylie mumble from the floor.

Yeah, well, Sophie thought, *neither are you.*

CHAPTER
Seven

The following week, Sophie was standing at her locker, when she felt a tap on her shoulder. She turned around — and shrieked.

A giant mule face with crossed eyes and buck teeth was hovering just inches away from her nose.

"Gooooo, Mules!" Kylie shouted from inside the head.

"Gosh, Kye, you scared me," Sophie said. She put a hand over her fast-beating heart.

Kylie pulled the costume off her head. "I know. It's frightening," she said. "Ms. Charge couldn't let me into the equipment room after school, so I had to get this now. It doesn't even fit in my locker. I'm going to have to carry it around until the game this afternoon. Of course," she added, eyeing Sophie's uniform, "it's no match for your outfit. Isn't that skirt against school regulations?"

Sophie blushed as she tugged at the hem of her pleated cheerleading skirt. Kylie was right. School rules said that skirts and shorts couldn't be more than two inches above the knee. But when Sophie held her hands at her sides, her skirt barely reached her fingertips.

"I guess they make an exception for cheerleading uniforms," she said unhappily. "Please don't make a big deal about it. It's embarrassing enough as it is."

If Sophie had ever had second thoughts about cheerleading, she was having them now. It was one thing to spend your afternoons tumbling and practicing cheers. It was another to show up for math class wearing a skirt so short it required matching underwear.

Kylie leaned against the locker next to Sophie's and stared across the hallway. "Look how cute he looks in a tie," she said dreamily.

Sophie didn't need to ask whom she was talking about. She glanced over at Scott. He had traded in his usual T-shirt and jeans for a blue button-down, khakis, and a yellow tie. The first big game of the season was that afternoon. Just as the cheerleaders wore their uniforms on game days to show their school spirit, the football players dressed up to show how serious they were about the game.

"Here I am, the love of his life, standing right across the hall," Kylie complained. "I can't believe he hasn't noticed me yet."

Sophie couldn't believe it, either. Kylie was kind of hard to miss. Especially when she was holding a two-foot-high mule head.

"Why don't you go say something to him?" she suggested.

"Like what? 'Marry me?'"

"I was thinking more like, 'Hi, how's it going?'" said Sophie.

Kylie frowned. "I can't just walk up and start talking to him." Suddenly, her face brightened. "Oh! But maybe I could pretend to drop something by his locker! And when I stood up, he'd be standing right there, and I could be, like, 'Hey!'"

"That's not a bad idea," Sophie said.

"You think?"

"Go get 'im, girl."

Kylie took a deep breath and started to head toward Scott's locker.

"Kye?" said Sophie.

Kylie turned. "What?"

"Maybe you should leave the mule head here."

"Oh. Right."

As Kylie set off to make her love connection, Sophie went back to searching for her math book in her locker.

"Hey, Sophie."

Sophie looked up. Joel was standing by her locker door. "How's it going?" he asked.

"Um, fine." *Dang!* Sophie thought. Of all the people in the school, Joel was the last person she wanted to see her in her cheerleading outfit.

"So, are you ready for your first game?" he asked.

She shrugged. Thinking about the game made her even more nervous. "Yeah, I guess. Whatever," she mumbled.

Joel's smile dimmed a notch. "Oh. Well, I just wanted to let you know I'll be there."

Joel was coming to the game? Joel was going to watch her cheer? Whenever she'd pictured herself actually cheering, it had always been in front of a faceless crowd. But of course, that was dumb. The people who would be at the game would be all kids she knew. Like Joel.

"Cool," Sophie said unenthusiastically.

Before Joel could reply, they were interrupted by a commotion across the hall. Sophie turned just in time to see Scott's books go flying from his hands as he tripped over Kylie, who was kneeling right in front of his locker.

Sophie and Joel winced.

"Oh!" Kylie sprang to grab one of the books at the same time Scott did. Their heads collided. As Scott put a hand to his bruised forehead, Kylie got hold of the book. "Here ya go," she said with a radiant smile.

Scott gingerly took the book. He quickly collected the others before Kylie could get to them and walked on down the hall, shaking his head.

A moment later, Kylie came stomping back over to Sophie's locker. Her face was crimson.

"That," she said, "did not go well."

"Let's get fired up!"
Clap-clap-clap-clap.
"We are fired up!"
Clap-clap-clap-clap.

As the football players took the field, the Meridian Middle School cheerleaders tried to get the crowd energized by clapping their hands.

"Really fired up!"
Clap-clap-clap-clap.

As she cheered, Sophie ran her eyes over the crowd in the bleachers. She told herself she wasn't looking for Joel. She was just looking. But when she spotted him sitting with a few other guys from their class, her stomach did a little flip.

"Let's go, Mules!"

Kylie stood to the side of the cheerleaders, wearing her huge mule head and a fuzzy brown jumpsuit. When the cheerleaders hit their final pose, she ran in, slid to a stop on one knee, and threw out her arms as if to say "Ta-da!"

One or two kids in the crowd clapped listlessly. Someone offered a thin whistle.

What's the point of having cheerleaders if no one cheers? Sophie thought unhappily. *And even if they do cheer, is it really going to make a difference?* Suddenly, she wondered what she was doing there at all. Maybe Kylie was right. Maybe she should have quit at the beginning.

Keisha yelled at the cheerleaders to get into formation again. For the next forty-five minutes, they ran through cheer after cheer. They did defense cheers when the other team had the ball and offense cheers when Meridian got it back.

Whenever Meridian did something good, the girls raised their arms and kicked their legs high.

The whole time, Sophie kept one anxious eye on Keisha. She didn't know much about football, and she was afraid she'd cheer for the wrong team if she wasn't careful.

By halftime, Sophie's voice was hoarse from shouting. Her cheeks hurt from forcing a smile she didn't really feel.

The Meridian marching band strode onto the field, playing a wobbly version of "Stars and Stripes Forever." A plump, curly-haired boy holding a pair of cymbals brought up the rear. Sophie didn't recognize him. She thought he must be a sixth-grader, new to the band. Every few steps he happily bashed the cymbals together, heedless of the music.

Watching the cymbals player, Sophie began to giggle. Suddenly, the whole situation seemed upside down. Shy Sophie had become a cheerleader. Stylie Kylie was a mule. And the cymbals player . . . well, she didn't know where he belonged, but it clearly wasn't in the band.

It was all like one big accident. The idea struck her as funny. At that moment, the cymbals crashed again, making Sophie giggle harder.

She glanced up at the stands and saw Joel laughing. He looked over and caught Sophie's eye, and she knew he'd noticed the cymbals player. They smiled, sharing the joke. Sophie surprised herself by giving him a little wave. He waved back.

Just then her eyes fell on Kylie. She was running in front of the bleachers, trying to get the crowd to do the wave. Everyone ignored her.

Sophie's smile faded. She couldn't see Kylie's face inside the mule head. But from her slumped shoulders, Sophie could tell she wasn't having a good time.

For the rest of the game, when she wasn't watching Keisha, Sophie watched Kylie. When Meridian got the ball, the mascot jumped up and down. She tried again to get the crowd to do the wave. But as the game wore on, Kylie jumped less and less. Soon her feet barely left the ground.

Meridian lost the game, 14–7. Sophie was headed over to commiserate with Kylie when she spotted her mother coming down the bleachers toward her.

"Mom!" said Sophie. "What are you doing here? I thought you weren't going to pick me up until five-thirty."

"I snuck out of work early," her mother confessed. "I left behind a whole stack of work. I didn't want to miss your first game."

Sophie's mother was a librarian at the local

college where her father worked as a dean. Both her parents took their jobs very seriously. They almost never missed work, even when they were sick.

"You were wonderful, sweetheart," her mother said, putting an arm around her. "All those high kicks. And some of those cheers were very . . . clever. Like little poems."

Sophie smiled. She had the feeling this was the first football game her mother had ever been to. Her parents weren't exactly the sports-going type.

Both her mother and father had been astonished when their shy, quiet daughter told them she'd made the cheerleading team. Astonished, and a little concerned. "Well, I always said you could do whatever you put your mind to," her father had blustered. "But it won't get in the way of your schoolwork now, will it?" "That's amazing, sweetie," her mother had said, not even bothering to hide her surprise. "Is that what you really want to do?" Sophie couldn't exactly blame them. She could hardly believe it herself.

So Sophie was surprised and pleased that her mother showed up at the game. She knew she was trying to be supportive.

"You were wonderful, too, Kylie," Sophie's mom added as Kylie walked up holding her mule head.

"Thanks, Mrs. Smith," Kylie said dispiritedly. "But I know I stank."

"Well, I don't know much about mascots, but I thought you were terrific. I'm taking you both out for ice cream to celebrate," said Sophie's mom.

Another surprise. Sophie's eyebrows shot up. Her parents hardly ever bought sweets. Their idea of a tasty dessert was fresh fruit and yogurt.

Her mother caught her look. "It's a treat," she said. "Don't tell your dad."

"Thanks, Mrs. Smith," said Kylie, "but I'm not really hungry. I think I'm just going to catch the late bus home."

"We can give you a ride, Kylie," Sophie's mom volunteered.

Kylie shook her head. "That's okay. See you, Soph."

"I'll call you later," Sophie said. She watched as Kylie shuffled away, her mascot head tucked under her arm. She knew Kylie was upset about the game, and she wanted to talk to her. But her mom seemed so excited about the treat she had planned. Sophie didn't want to leave her hanging.

"Shall we go?" said Mrs. Smith.

Sophie nodded. "Ice cream, here we come!"

CHAPTER
Eight

The next two games didn't go any better for the football team — or for Kylie. Though she wore herself out running up and down in front of the crowd, trying to get them to do waves, they mostly ignored her.

Sophie could tell her friend was growing more and more discouraged. She started to dread game days, more for Kylie's sake than anything. At the same time, she worried that Kylie would quit. Sophie didn't want to be stuck going to games without her.

Then, on the afternoon of the fourth game, Kylie didn't show up.

Sophie watched for her while the cheerleaders warmed up, and through their first several cheers. When Kylie still wasn't there by the second quarter of the game, Sophie started to realize she wasn't coming.

But by then the Mules were ahead. Sophie forgot about Kylie for a moment. It looked like the football team might actually have a chance at winning a game.

The Mules scored a touchdown. The crowd cheered. Sophie kicked her leg up by her ear to show how happy she was.

Keisha gave them the signal to take their places for another cheer.

"Are. You. Ready. For. M-M-S.
Are you ready
To be challenged
By none but the best!"

They were halfway through the cheer when Sophie realized that some people in the crowd were laughing.

Are they laughing at us? she wondered.

She looked around. Kylie, wearing her mule costume, had finally arrived. She was standing behind the cheerleaders, trying to follow along with the cheer. But since she hadn't learned it, her moves were all one step behind.

The cheerleaders finished their cheer with high kicks and cartwheels. Out of the corner of her eye, Sophie saw Kylie trying to lift her leg into the air. The huge mask made it difficult. Her wobbly kick looked especially funny.

The crowd laughed again.

Encouraged, Kylie put her hands on the ground and kicked her feet in the air in one of her lopsided cartwheels.

"Go, Mules!" someone shouted.

Sophie glanced over and saw Keisha watching Kylie. She had her hands on her hips and was frowning.

For the rest of the game, Kylie cheered right alongside the cheerleaders. When she didn't know the moves, she made them up. The crowd seemed to love her. They laughed and hollered every time she started dancing.

By the end of the game, the Mules had won, 21–6.

Afterward, Sophie was collecting her pom-poms when Kylie walked up. She was holding the mascot head under one arm. Her cheeks were pink and the curls at her temples were damp with sweat. "Can you unzip me?" she asked Sophie. "This costume is crazy hot."

Sophie unzipped the back of the furry suit. "Where were you at the beginning of the game?" she asked. "I was looking for you."

"I lost my head."

"You what?"

"I lost my mule head. I accidentally left it somewhere."

"Where?"

"In the janitor's closet in the basement."

Sophie looked at her. "You mean 'accidentally' on purpose?"

Kylie gave her a sheepish smile. "Yeah. I guess I thought if I didn't have the head, I wouldn't be able to come to the games anymore. Lucky for me, the janitor found it and brought it to Ms. Charge. And Ms. Charge *made sure* I got to the game."

Sophie giggled. "I'll bet she did. I'm glad you made it, though. You were really good. Everyone was laughing."

Kylie grinned. "Yeah, they were, weren't they? It was actually pretty fun acting so goofy. I figured I already looked so dumb, I had nothing to lose."

Over the next couple of weeks, Kylie made Sophie teach her some of the cheers. Then at the games, she mixed them all up, adding her own crazy moves.

She was a hit. The crowd cheered even louder when Kylie came onto the field.

Even at school people started to say "Go, Mules!" whenever they saw Kylie. Sophie thought it was kind of embarrassing. But Kylie just laughed. Sophie could tell she liked the attention. Kylie liked most kinds of attention.

Sophie herself was actually starting to like cheerleading. At practices, Keisha and the other girls treated her as part of the group. She'd become the best flyer, nailing the stunts almost as soon as Ms. Charge taught them. The games were better, too. Sophie didn't have to keep reminding herself to smile — it had started to come naturally.

Sophie couldn't tell if all the cheering actually made a difference to the game. But something seemed to be working. By the middle of October, the Meridian Middle School football team had started to come around from their losing streak.

One afternoon, after winning another game, Sophie and the other cheerleaders were in the locker room, when Keisha walked up. "Hey, Bitsy."

"Hey, Keisha!" said Sophie. "Good game, right?"

"Yeah, it was good. So, I wanted to let you know, I'm having a party next Saturday," Keisha said. "You can come. All the cheerleaders are invited."

"Really?" Sophie's eyes widened. "Great, I'll ask my —" She stopped herself. Maybe it wasn't cool to say you had to ask your mom. "I'll be there," she finished.

Keisha nodded. "I'll e-mail you the address. By the way, Bitsy, your hair looks really good these days. See ya." With a little wave, she walked back over to where Courtney, Trisha, and Kate were waiting for her. Sophie watched as they picked up their bags and left.

A few lockers down, Alyssa was folding her uniform into a gym bag. Sophie turned to her, excited. "So you're going to Keisha's party?" she asked.

Alyssa shrugged. "Probably not. Next Saturday is Renee's parents' anniversary. She's got to baby-sit her little brother and sister. I told her I'd help out."

Alyssa was choosing babysitting over a party at Keisha's house? Sophie stared at her in disbelief. "Wow, too bad for Renee," she said. "But she could probably get someone else to help out, couldn't she?"

"She probably could," said Alyssa, "but I already told her I would. I don't back out on my friends just because Keisha snaps her fingers." There was an edge to her voice.

Alyssa zipped up her bag. "See you tomorrow!"

she said. Swinging her bag over her shoulder, she headed out the door.

Well, Sophie thought, *whatever Alyssa's problem with Keisha is, it has nothing to do with me.* She smiled and hugged herself. She was invited to a party at an eighth-grader's house. And not just any eighth-grader, but Keisha Reyes, the most popular girl in school!

"Serious shivers!" Sophie murmured.

"What's serious shivers?" Kylie asked, walking up behind her.

Sophie turned to her with a grin. "Guess what? We're invited to a party at Keisha's house!"

CHAPTER
Nine

All week, Sophie carried the words around with her like a charm. "You are invited." They made her feel different — prettier, more interesting. It was as if she had been cast under a magic spell and transformed into someone cool.

She wasn't the only one who noticed. Lately, kids Sophie hardly knew were saying hi to her in the halls. And not just anyone, but popular kids, the ones who had hardly even looked at her last year. But last year, Sophie reminded herself, she would have blushed and ducked away. The new, cool Sophie was much more outgoing.

"Are you running for class president or something?" Kylie asked her as they walked to class on Thursday.

"What are you talking about?" said Sophie.

"You've been saying hi to practically every person we pass. It's like you're on a campaign."

Sophie frowned and shook her hair back from her eyes. "They said hi to me first," she retorted. "I'm just saying hi back."

Kylie gave her a funny look. "Right. Whatever. So, I was wondering, do you want to come over after school today? I figured since you don't have cheerleading practice you'd have time. There's some stuff I want to get ready for the game tomorrow."

The game the next day was with Northwest Middle School, Meridian's main rival. Ms. Charge had given the cheerleaders the day off, with instructions to carbo-load and get lots of rest. Sometimes Sophie thought Ms. Charge forgot that they were just cheering and not actually playing the game.

"I'd like to," Sophie told Kylie apologetically. "But I can't. My mom and I are going shopping together this afternoon."

Ever since she'd gotten the invitation to Keisha's party, Sophie had been aware of a new problem. She had nothing to wear. Normally, she took all her fashion problems straight to Kylie. But Kylie didn't really seem interested in talking about the party. Every time Sophie brought it up, she changed the subject.

Not that she'd had much chance to bring it up.

Sophie had hardly seen Kylie all week. Twice when Sophie had gone to meet her at her locker for lunch, Kylie hadn't been there. So Sophie had sat with some of the other cheerleaders instead. She'd always scooted over to make room for Kylie when she finally arrived in the cafeteria. But each time Kylie had walked right by as if she didn't see her.

Sophie knew something was wrong. But Kylie wasn't saying anything, so neither did Sophie. She didn't want to make a big deal out of it.

In the meantime, Keisha's party was in two days. Sophie was starting to realize that if she was going to find an outfit she would have to take matters into her own hands.

"You're shopping with your mom? That's cool," said Kylie. "Maybe she could drop you off at my house afterward. You could have dinner with us. My mom's trying to close a deal on a house, which means we'll probably be ordering Chinese."

"I can't," Sophie said with a sigh. "I really need to catch up on my homework. I've been so tired after practice this week, I haven't had time to get to it all."

"Oh, okay. Well, do you think you could help me after school tomorrow? I'm going to have a lot of stuff to carry."

They had arrived at Sophie's Spanish classroom. Sophie paused at the door and smiled. "Sure thing," she said to Kylie.

"How about these, sweetheart?" Sophie's mom said. She held up a pair of shorts for Sophie's inspection. Each pocket had a big calico heart stitched onto it.

Sophie cringed. They had been browsing through the store for half an hour, and so far her mother had managed to pick out twenty things that would have been absolutely perfect if Sophie were a six-year-old.

"They have rules about shorts at school," she reminded her mom. *Rules about not looking like a total dork,* she added to herself.

Sophie was starting to worry. The department store would close in an hour, and she still hadn't found the perfect outfit for Keisha's party. Plus, she had an extra errand she needed to do without her mother around.

"Actually, Mom, it might take me a little while," Sophie said. "Do you want to go to the shoe department? I can meet you there."

"Are you sure? You'll be okay here?" asked Mrs. Smith, a twinkle forming in her eye at the mention of shoes. Sophie's mom loved shoes. She owned pairs and pairs of loafers, clogs, sandals, and flats, all in unthrilling shades of brown, black, and beige. It was a great mystery to Sophie that someone could have such an enormous shoe collection and still not own a single interesting pair.

When her mom was gone, Sophie began quickly to riffle through the clothes on the racks. She considered a T-shirt with a graphic of a cat, then put it back. She looked at a denim miniskirt with a frayed hem, a jeweled camouflage tank top . . . nothing seemed right. Sophie wished Kylie were with her. Kylie could plunge her hands into the sale rack and pull out a dazzling outfit. She was a magician that way.

Then Sophie rounded a corner and saw it. A soft jade-colored sweater, as thin as tissue paper. It was paired with dark gray jeans that had a design in rhinestones on the back pocket.

"Please let them come in my size," she whispered aloud.

They did. The jeans fit like they'd been made just for her, and the sweater was the softest thing she'd ever felt against her skin. It was the perfect outfit for Keisha's party.

When she looked at the price tags her heart nearly skipped a beat. The jeans were almost a hundred dollars. The sweater, which turned out to be made of cashmere, cost even more.

Sophie had never spent that much money on anything in her life. She couldn't imagine spending it on a single outfit. And yet . . .

She didn't let herself think about it. Her mind was blank as she walked over to the cash register and took out her credit card. She watched numbly as the cashier rang up her purchases.

As soon as the clothes were in a shopping bag, Sophie felt better. It was done, and there was no going back. Now she had just one more errand.

The cosmetics counters were located on the first floor, just across from the women's shoe department. Sophie went to the counter at the far end of the store, away from the shoes. She hovered in front of the display case, waiting for the saleswoman to notice her.

"Can I help you?" the woman asked at last. She had bright red lips and silvery eye shadow.

"I'd like some mascara," Sophie told her.

"Which kind?"

Sophie was confused. "The kind that goes on eyelashes?"

The woman's red lips pinched in what Sophie took to be a smile. "What would you like it to *do*? Condition? Thicken? Lengthen?"

"Oh, lengthen," Sophie said quickly. "And thicken, maybe."

"That kind comes in six colors. Soft black, mid-night black, blue black, brown —"

"Soft black is fine," Sophie interrupted. She wished the woman would hurry. Her mother could show up any minute.

The woman took a slender box from beneath the counter. "That will be seventeen dollars and twelve cents."

Sophie swallowed. She knew it would have been cheaper to buy mascara from the drugstore. But she couldn't think of a reason to give her mother for going to the drugstore. And besides, the saleswoman was already ringing up her purchase.

Sophie took out her credit card.

A few moments later, she found her mother in the shoe department, surrounded by open boxes.

"Done already?" Mrs. Smith said. She stuck out her feet for Sophie's inspection. She wore a tan loafer on one foot, a brown one on the other. "What do you think? Tan or brown?"

Sophie thought they looked equally boring. "Brown, I guess."

Mrs. Smith sighed. "I really shouldn't get anything. So what did you buy?" she asked, spotting Sophie's shopping bag.

"Not much. Just some jeans and a sweater."

"That's all?" said her mother. "You're just like

your father. So practical. I should take a lesson from you. I really don't need any more shoes." She turned her attention back to her feet, then sighed and told the salesman, "I guess I won't get anything today."

She slid her feet back into her own shoes and watched as he packed up the boxes and took them away. She gave Sophie a little regretful smile. "They were too expensive. I guess we can't buy everything we want just because we want it, can we?"

"No," said Sophie, trying to swallow around the lump of guilt in her throat. "I guess we can't."

Sophie blinked her eyes and scanned the crowd assembling on the bleachers. She was looking for Joel. He had been to every football game this season, and Sophie figured he wouldn't miss the big game against Northwest. But she hadn't seen him all afternoon.

Sophie blinked a few more times. Her eyelashes felt like they were wearing little sweaters. Just before the game she'd been in the girls' bathroom, practicing putting mascara on with Trisha and Kate. They were impressed by the brand she'd bought, and Sophie had congratulated herself on getting such a good kind. She hoped Joel would get a chance to see her with her new lengthened and thickened lashes.

I'll have to tell Kylie, Sophie thought. *Maybe she won't think mascara is so gross when she sees how good I look.*

Kylie! Sophie's heavy eyelashes flew open. She'd told Kylie she would meet her in the equipment room after school. But then she'd started talking about makeup with Trisha and Kate, and she'd forgotten all about it. It was too late to go now. The football players were lining up for the kickoff, and Keisha was already signaling the cheerleaders to get ready for their first cheer.

The game got off to a close start. In the first quarter, Northwest scored two touchdowns, and Meridian scored one. But in the second quarter, Meridian's kicker missed a field goal. The receiver fumbled two important passes. Northwest started to pull ahead.

At halftime, Northwest was winning, 24–7. The cheerleaders were pulling out all their best cheers. But as the team continued to fall behind, the crowd seemed to grow more and more discouraged.

"Where's Kylie?" a couple of the other cheerleaders asked Sophie. Each time Sophie shrugged, fighting an uneasy feeling. She wondered why Kylie had wanted her help in the equipment room. Was it her fault that Kylie wasn't at the game now?

Halftime was almost over when Sophie spotted

Joel standing at the edge of the field. She waved and started to head over to ask if he'd seen Kylie. Joel seemed to look right at her, but he didn't wave back. A second later, he turned and walked away.

Sophie stopped in her tracks. Had he not seen her?

Just then, Kylie arrived. She was wearing her mule costume and carrying what looked like a large piece of white paperboard.

She marched over until she was standing right in front of the bleachers. She turned to face the crowd and held the sign up in front of her.

Kylie's back was to the cheerleaders, so Sophie couldn't see what the sign said. But a few kids who were sitting in front read it out loud. "MULES RULES."

Kylie tossed the sign away. There was another sign underneath it.

"NUMBER ONE," the kids read. "BE COOL."

More people had started to look. Kylie tossed that sign away and held up the next one.

"NUMBER TWO: DON'T DROOL." Several kids laughed at that one.

"NUMBER THREE," they joined in reading, "CHEER LIKE FOOLS . . ."

Kylie held up another sign.

"FOR YOUR SCHOOL!"

Kylie threw that away and held up the last sign. "CUZ THE MULES RULE!" everyone in the bleachers shouted.

Kylie threw down the sign, put her hands on the ground, and bucked her feet in the air.

The crowd cheered. They made so much noise that the fans from the other team turned to see what they were yelling about.

For the rest of the game, whenever there was an important point to be scored, Kylie held up the MULES RULES sign, and the crowd roared. When the Mules made a touchdown, Kylie did a crazy dance and bucked her feet in the air, and everyone yelled, "MULES RULE!"

The only people who didn't seem to love Kylie were some of the cheerleaders. From the look on Keisha's face, Sophie could tell she was getting seriously annoyed.

The team seemed to respond to the cheers from the crowd. By the end of the game, the Mules had managed to come from behind. The final score was 24–21. Northwest won by three points.

"That was cool, Kylie," Renee said after the game as the cheerleaders collected their things. "Mules Rules. That's really clever."

Kylie was sitting on the bleachers. She had taken her mask off and was using one of the paperboard signs to fan her face. "I'm glad you think so," she said coolly. She didn't sound like she meant it.

Sophie wished for once that Kylie would try to be friendlier to the cheerleaders. Sometimes she acted like they were playing on different teams.

"No, really," Angie piped up, oblivious to Kylie's attitude. "I think you made a big difference. The team really came back with all those people cheering."

"She didn't make a difference," said Keisha, giving Angie a withering look. "We *lost* the game."

Angie seemed to shrink.

"But we didn't lose by much," pointed out Alyssa.

Just then, Ms. Charge hustled over. "Terrific, Kylie!" she boomed. "That is *just* the sort of spirit and creativity we need on this team. Well done! But next game, be on time."

"Thanks, Ms. Charge," Kylie said sweetly. "I will." She looked directly at Keisha as she spoke.

Keisha narrowed her eyes. Then she turned and stalked away. Courtney, Trisha, and Kate trailed after her.

When the group had broken up, Sophie sat

down next to Kylie. "Um, when did you make all those signs?"

"Last night, when you were shopping with your mom." Kylie gave her a steady look. "Joel came over and helped me. He also helped me carry them *today*, when you *didn't* meet me in the equipment room."

Sophie flushed. "Kye, I'm sorry about that. I . . . got busy doing something."

"Yeah, I guess you're really busy these days."

"It's just that . . ."

Sophie wanted to explain how being a cheerleader was more complicated than she'd imagined. You had to say hi to the right people in the halls and have the right clothes and nice eyelashes. And when girls like Trisha and Kate wanted to hang out, you couldn't just say no. Sometimes it was hard to keep track of everything you were supposed to do.

Instead, she said, "It's like the STAR thing Ms. Charge always talks about. You know, studies and being part of the team and training and all — I've got a lot going on."

"Did you ever notice," Kylie said slowly, "that STAR backward spells RATS?"

Sophie stared at her. Suddenly, she was angry. Why should Kylie get all bent out of shape just because once — just once — Sophie hadn't showed up? What about all the times Kylie had flaked out on Sophie, or gone back on her word, and Sophie hadn't said a thing? Well, she had something to say now.

"You're just jealous that I made the team and you didn't," she told Kylie.

Kylie drew back like she'd been slapped. Without a word, she stood up and started to collect her things.

But there were too many things to carry. When she tried to pick up the signboards, she dropped her mask. She grabbed the mask, and more signs slipped from her grip.

Sophie watched her, filled with regret. As soon as the words had left her mouth, she wanted to take them back — even if they were true.

"Let me help you," she said contritely.

"I don't need your help," Kylie snapped.

Sophie picked up the signboards anyway. With her assistance, everything was soon precariously balanced in Kylie's arms.

Kylie started to leave. A few steps away, she paused and turned. "Soph."

"What?"

"You'd better wash that stuff off your eyes

before your mom sees you. It's all down your face. You look like a raccoon."

Sophie rubbed a finger under her eye. It came off black. "Thanks," she said.

Kylie nodded and walked away. Sophie watched her go. Even angry, Kylie still had her back.

CHAPTER
Ten

The large brick house was set back from the street, in the middle a rolling green lawn. In the dim twilight, Sophie thought it looked like a great rocky island floating in an emerald sea.

She double-checked the number on the invitation: 2014 Rightside Drive. This was it.

Sophie let her father drive past it. When they reached the house next door, she said, "This is it, Dad!"

Mr. Smith steered the station wagon over to the curb. Sophie hadn't wanted him to stop right in front of Keisha's house. She was keenly aware of how dirty the Smiths' old station wagon seemed compared to the shiny SUVs and sedans parked in the driveways of the neighboring houses.

Normally, Sophie didn't pay attention to things

like cars. But somehow she had the feeling that Keisha did.

She leaned over and gave her father a peck on the cheek. "Thanks, Dad."

"Thanks, Mr. Smith," Kylie and Joel echoed from the backseat.

"Have fun," Mr. Smith said. "I'll be back at eleven to pick you up."

The kids got out of the car. Sophie waved good-bye to her dad, then turned and started up the walkway of the house in front of them.

As soon as Mr. Smith pulled away, she began to cut across the lawn toward Keisha's house.

"What are you doing?" asked Joel. "I thought you said it was this one."

"I made a mistake," Sophie said, holding up the invitation. "It's actually 2014, not 2016. It was hard to read the numbers in the dark."

It had been Kylie's idea to invite Joel to come to the party with them. After their argument the day before, Sophie had had to beg her to come. Kylie had finally agreed, but only if Joel came, too.

Not that Sophie minded. She hoped Joel noticed how nice she looked in her new clothes. She had added a silver necklace with a heart charm, and she'd worn her best sandals, the ones with the wraparound straps, even though the night was cool. Sophie had decided to forget the mascara. She didn't want to find it smeared all over her face halfway through the party.

Joel and Kylie followed Sophie across the grass. The sprinklers had been on, and Sophie could feel the cuffs of her almost-one-hundred-dollar jeans getting soaked.

When they reached the front door, Sophie rang the doorbell. A little girl with black hair like Keisha's answered the door. She stared at them without saying anything.

"Hello!" Kylie said, bending over to smile at her. "Who're you?"

The little girl stuck out her tongue and ran away. A moment later a woman came to the door.

"I'm sorry," she told Sophie and her friends. "That was Missy. She really wanted to answer the door. I'm Mrs. Reyes. Come on in." Mrs. Reyes stood aside to let them pass. "The rest of the kids are downstairs. Just go down the hall and you'll find the stairwell."

The Reyeses' entire basement had been converted into a huge rec room. On one side of the room, a group of eighth-grade boys were sprawled out on couches, watching music videos on a widescreen TV. On the other side of the room, the girls were clustered around a built-in bar. Some perched on bar stools, while others stood. They nibbled on chips and snacks from bowls that sat on the counter.

Trisha and Kate were there, of course. And so was Courtney, wearing more than her usual amount of makeup. The twins, hair plaited in matching French braids, sat on either side of Keisha. Amy, Angie, and Joy hovered together over a bowl of corn chips, looking thrilled to be there. Alyssa and Renee were the only cheerleaders missing.

The girls all looked up when Sophie, Kylie, and Joel walked in. Sophie saw Trisha lean over to Courtney and whisper something in her ear. Courtney smirked.

Keisha was sitting on a bar stool sipping a can of soda with a straw. She watched as Sophie walked over to her.

"Hey, guys," Sophie said to the cheerleaders. "Hey, Keisha."

"Hi, Bitsy," Keisha said coolly. "Glad you could make it." She glanced over Sophie's shoulder at Kylie and Joel. "I guess you brought the whole Mule train with you."

A few of the cheerleaders snickered.

Sophie hesitated. As the cheerleaders went

back to their conversation, she pulled Joel and Kylie aside. "Maybe you should go hang out with the guys," she suggested to Joel in a whisper.

Joel looked over at the boys. They were all eighth-grade football players. " I don't know any of those guys," he said.

Sophie started to feel nervous. She wanted to talk to Joel. But he wasn't exactly going to fit in with the cheerleaders. "Well, what else are you going to do?" she hissed. "You can't stand around chitchatting with the girls."

Joel gave her a funny look. Immediately, she was sorry she'd said it that way. "I think we should bail," he said.

"But we just got here!" Sophie protested.

"I'm with Joel," Kylie agreed. "I'm getting bad vibes."

"You can't leave yet, Kylie. Scott Hersh is here." Sophie pointed over to a couch where Scott was slumped, his eyes glued to the TV.

Kylie's eyes flicked toward him. "I don't like him anymore," she told Sophie. "I don't know why I ever did. He's just a dumb jock."

Sophie stared at her in surprise. Since when had Kylie stopped liking Scott? "Well, we can't leave now. It would be rude," she argued. "And besides, my dad's not coming to pick us up until eleven."

"We don't have to wait for your dad," Kylie said. "We can walk to the Esplanade and call one of our parents to pick us up." The Esplanade was an outdoor mall with upscale stores and a fancy restaurant. It was only about half a mile from Keisha's house.

Sophie didn't want to leave. She'd been waiting for this party all week. And Keisha would think she was weird for leaving five minutes after she arrived. So she said the last thing she could think of to get her friends to stay. "You guys are being lame."

Joel looked at Sophie silently. Then he said, "Come on, Kylie." A minute later, the two had disappeared up the stairs.

Sophie wandered back over to the cheerleaders.

"Where're your friends?" Keisha asked.

"They had to leave."

"Too bad," Keisha replied. "Kylie probably just left to get attention. She wants everyone to miss her."

"Boo-hoo," Courtney said sarcastically.

"So, Bitsy, are you, like, best friends with Mulegirl?" Keisha wanted to know.

"Why?" Sophie said carefully.

"Just asking. I think she looks really stupid at the games, dancing around like that and messing up the cheers. It makes everyone look bad."

"It does?" said Sophie. "But isn't that what she's supposed to do?"

"Last year the mascot just ran around and got the crowd to do the wave and things. He was a guy. I think it's kind of weird for a girl to be a mascot, don't you?"

"Maybe." Sophie couldn't see how it mattered whether there was a guy or a girl in the costume, since no one could see who it was, anyway. But she wasn't going to say so to Keisha.

Sophie nibbled on a handful of snack mix and listened halfheartedly as the other girls gossiped about boys at school. She couldn't stop thinking about the way Joel had looked at her right before he left, as if he were making some kind of decision about her. She half wished that she had left the party with him and Kylie.

But I'm here now, she told herself. *I might as well enjoy it.* She tried to tune back in to the conversation.

The girls were admiring Keisha's bracelet. "I always wanted a charm bracelet like that," Joy gushed.

Sophie nodded. "Serious shivers," she agreed.

Keisha looked at her. "What?"

"Serious shivers," Sophie said, suddenly very aware that everyone was looking at her. "You know, when something's so cool it sends chills down your spine."

"You're cute, Bitsy," said Keisha. Then she turned and looked over at the boys. "Those guys are being lame," she said.

She stood from her stool and picked up a bowl of cheese puffs. The girls watched as she walked up behind Dominick, who was slouched on a couch, and dumped the bowl over his head.

Dominick let out a whoop. He reached out, grabbed a bowl of chips from the table, and flung it backward into Keisha's face.

Suddenly, as if the invisible levee separating them had burst, the boys and the girls were all mixed up. The girls took bowls of ammunition from the bar and began to fling chips, candies, and pretzels at the boys. The boys were scooping up handfuls and throwing them back. A variety of snack foods were getting crushed into the carpet.

Sophie hovered by the bar. She couldn't imagine how to insert herself into the scene. She also didn't want to get cheese puffs squashed on her new cashmere sweater.

Jake, who was one of the biggest guys on the

team, accidentally stepped on the TV remote and broke it. To Sophie's amazement, Keisha laughed. Sophie's parents would have been furious if her friends made a mess in her house and broke things, but Keisha didn't seem to care at all.

After a while, Scott Hersh, who had been sitting silently on the couch, extracted himself from the fray. He wandered over to the bar and took a can of soda from the fridge. Then he scooped up a handful of corn chips from one of the few bowls remaining on the bar.

Sophie took a chip, too. They stood side by side, munching and watching the rest of the kids. Sophie tried to think of something to say.

"It would be good if they had some dip," Scott said after a moment.

Sophie looked at him.

"You know, for the chips."

"You should try the potato chips," Sophie told him. "They have a, um, diplike flavor."

Diplike flavor? She could have kicked herself. She sounded like some loser in a bad TV commercial.

Scott took a chip from the bowl and popped it in his mouth. "Diplike," he agreed.

Sophie finally thought of something to say. "So how's football going?" *Not brilliant,* she told herself. *But better than "diplike flavor."*

112

"'S'okay," Scott said. There was a pause. "Um, how's cheerleading?" he asked.

"It's okay. Cheerful."

He laughed. Sophie felt a tiny surge of confidence.

"So how come you're standing over here?" asked Scott

"How come *you're* standing over here?" countered Sophie.

Scott looked over at the food fight. "I dunno. Quieter, I guess."

"Yeah." It was starting to dawn on Sophie that Scott wasn't as stuck-up as she'd thought. He was just shy — like Sophie.

"I've seen you guys practicing out on the field," Scott told her. "You're pretty strong for someone so small."

"Thanks," said Sophie, "I think."

"No, really," said Scott. "I've seen you do back handsprings and stuff. Where did you learn to do all that?"

"I started taking gymnastics classes in first grade," Sophie told him. "And then I just kept on going, I guess. I only stopped last year."

"Why'd you quit?"

Sophie shrugged. "My coach told me that if I was going to keep doing it, I had to get serious. You know, practice four hours a day and go to national tournaments and all that. I decided it was too much. I just wanted to be a normal kid."

"Yeah," Scott said. "I get that. I mean, don't get me wrong. I love football and all. But sometimes when it's really hot out and Coach is making us run sprints until we want to puke, I think, *dang*, I could be inside playing video games right now."

Sophie laughed. They ate more chips and talked about sports and school. Sophie was surprised to find that Scott was funny and friendly. In fact, he was easier to talk to than Keisha and some of the other cheerleaders.

She would have to tell Kylie he wasn't a dumb jock at all. *Good thing I stayed at the party,* Sophie thought. *Otherwise, Kylie might never know.*

After a while, Courtney walked over to them. She was wearing so much lip gloss her mouth look shellacked.

"Why are you all the way over here, Scott?" Courtney asked, giving him a glossy pout. She grabbed his hands and tried to pull him off the stool he was sitting on. "You should come hang out."

"No, thanks," Scott said pleasantly. He withdrew his hands. "I'm okay here."

Courtney looked surprised for a second. She

glanced from Scott to Sophie, and her eyes narrowed. Then, with a toss of her pumpkin-colored hair, she turned and flounced back over to the rest of the kids.

Later, when Sophie was home in bed, she went over the evening in her mind. After everyone had calmed down from the cheese puffs attack, Keisha had organized a game of Truth or Dare. She'd dared Dominick to call Alison Martin, a shy, quiet girl in their class, and tell her he loved her. He'd dialed information so the Martins wouldn't see Keisha's number on caller ID, but Alison turned out not to be home. Then Dominick had dared Jake to eat a raw egg, which Keisha happily fetched from the refrigerator upstairs. When he'd completed his dare, Jake, looking a little green, had dared Trisha to kiss Scott. Trisha told everyone she couldn't because she had a cold, and even though no one believed her, they didn't make her do it. When it was her turn, Sophie had said "Truth," and when Amy asked her how many boys she'd kissed, she lied and said one.

All in all, Sophie thought it had been one of the most exciting evenings of her life. She couldn't wait to tell Kylie about it.

CHAPTER
Eleven

On Monday, Sophie sat in her sixth-period math class, struggling to concentrate. As her teacher wrote out a problem on the board, Sophie dutifully copied it into her notebook. But her mind was on Kylie and Joel.

When Sophie had called Kylie on Sunday to tell her about the party, Kylie barely seemed to listen. Even when she mentioned Scott, Kylie just said, "Hmm." Then Kylie had launched into a description of her evening with Joel.

When they got to the Esplanade, they hadn't called their parents right away, she told Sophie. Instead they'd walked around, ate ice cream, and looked in the shops. That's when they discovered the wedding party being photographed in the courtyard outside a ritzy restaurant. Kylie and Joel had spent the rest of the night lurking in the background, seeing how many wedding photos they could sneak into.

"The bride and groom were getting their picture taken," Kylie said over the phone, practically choking with laughter, "and Joel was standing in the background pretending to pick his nose."

Sophie laughed when Kylie told her about it. On Monday, when Kylie and Joel rehashed their evening over lunch, she pretended to be amused. But by Tuesday they were still talking about it, and Sophie was starting to get annoyed.

It wasn't *that* funny, she fumed as she copied history notes off the board. In fact, when you thought about it, it was pretty immature. What about the poor bride and groom who would get their pictures back from the photographer and see Joel picking his nose in the background?

But the poor bride and groom weren't really what bothered Sophie. What bugged her most was that Kylie and Joel had had so much fun without her.

Did Joel like Kylie? Did Kylie like Joel?

She didn't think so. Kylie was her best friend. She would have told Sophie if she liked Joel.

Then again, Sophie thought uneasily, *I didn't tell Kylie that I liked him.*

As she mulled this over, Sophie felt something nudge her elbow. She looked over and saw Melissa, the girl in the next seat, passing her a note. Melissa rolled her eyes toward the back of the room. Kate was giving Sophie an urgent look from the back row.

A note from Kate! Suddenly, Sophie felt better. She didn't need Kylie and Joel. She was friends with one of the most popular girls in the seventh grade.

Casting a quick glance at the teacher to make sure she wasn't looking, Sophie unfolded the note. Kate had written,

Sophie, Do you ♥ *Scott Hersh? FF, Kate*

What?! Sophie turned and looked at Kate with astonishment. Kate nodded for Sophie to write her back.

NO!!! Sophie wrote. She underlined it four times. Then she added, *Who told you that? FF, Sophie.*

She refolded the note and passed it to Melissa, who passed it to the guy behind her, who passed it to Kate.

Sophie's thoughts churned as she waited for Kate's reply. Were people talking about her and Scott? What were they saying?

A moment later the note came back.

It's so obvious. Everyone saw you flirting with him

at Keisha's party. Kate had drawn a bunch of little hearts around "flirting."

Sophie hesitated. Had she been flirting with Scott? She didn't think so. How could you be flirting with someone you didn't even like? Then again, Sophie didn't know anything about flirting. Was it possible she had been flirting without even knowing it?

At last she wrote, *We're just friends. I don't <u>like him</u> like him.*

Cool, Kate wrote back. *FYI, everyone is getting together at Courtney's to get ready for the Halloween dance. B there or B square.*

The Halloween dance was two weeks away. Kylie had been talking about it practically since *last* Halloween. She wouldn't tell anyone what her costume was going to be, not even Sophie.

Sophie and Kylie always got ready for Halloween together. *Then again,* Sophie thought, rereading Kate's note, *she definitely did not want to be square.*

She folded the note and put it in her pocket. She wanted to think more about it. She was going to have to figure out what to do.

It turned out she didn't have to. Every day at cheerleading practice Sophie waited for Courtney to mention the party at her house before the Halloween dance. But Courtney never did.

Finally, Sophie decided the party must have been canceled. It was just as well. Now she didn't have to make up an excuse for why she couldn't go.

On the night of the dance, Sophie and Kylie got ready at Kylie's house. "What do you think?" Kylie asked, turning away from the mirror. She was wearing a ruffled skirt, red lipstick, and a giant basket of plastic fruit tied to her head with a scarf.

"You look like one of those gift baskets my dad gets from work at Christmastime," Sophie told her.

"I'm Carmen Miranda," said Kylie. Carmen Miranda was one of Kylie's favorite actresses from the old black-and-white movies.

"*I* know that," said Sophie. "I'm just not sure anyone *else* will. Carmen Miranda didn't wear a basket on her head. She just wore fruit. And besides, she was alive, like, a million years ago."

Kylie turned back to the mirror and considered herself. Going over to her closet, she rummaged around and came up with a crumpled red ribbon. She tied it to the basket handle. "Voilà. *Now* I'm a gift basket."

Sophie fiddled with her stocking cap. At the last minute, she'd decided to be a green M&M. She was wearing a green cap and a long-sleeved green shirt

120

with the letters M&M stenciled on. It was Sophie's kind of costume. Subtle, she thought, but clever.

The dance was being held in the school cafeteria, a low-ceilinged room with small windows and a grubby gray floor. The dance committee had done their best to give it some atmosphere by hanging orange-and-black crepe paper streamers and placing smoking buckets of dry ice around the sides. Music blared from huge speakers set up in the corners.

Several kids turned to look when Sophie and Kylie walked in the door. A few of them laughed when they saw Kylie's costume. Kylie held her fruit high and smiled like a queen.

Sophie and Kylie agreed they should make a loop and look for people they knew. Halfway around the room, Sophie spotted Alyssa and Renee, dressed in disco outfits and neon-pink wigs. They were standing with a few kids from the student council. She went over to them.

"Hi!" Alyssa and Renee shouted over the music.

"Hey!" said Sophie. "Are you having fun?"

"Yeah!" said Alyssa. "The music is great!"

"Where's everyone else?" Sophie asked.

Alyssa and Renee shrugged and shook their

heads. They hadn't seen any of the other cheer-leaders.

Sophie told them she'd see them later and caught up with Kylie. They found Joel standing in a corner by the door with a few guys from the soccer team. He had Ace bandages wrapped over his clothes and around his head to look like a mummy.

"Let me guess," he said when he saw Kylie. "Carmen Miranda."

"Good guess!" said Sophie. "How do you know Carmen Miranda?"

Joel shrugged. "I like old movies."

"Good guess," Kylie agreed, "but wrong." She pointed to the bow. "Gift basket. It was Sophie's idea," she said when Joel chuckled.

"Good idea," Joel said to Sophie, who blushed. He looked at her green cap and shirt. "What are you? Green with envy?"

"A green M&M."

"Oh," said Joel. "Right." He didn't laugh.

A slow song came on. Around them boys and girls started to pair off. One of the guys from the soccer team asked Kylie to dance, and they moved out to the dance floor.

Sophie stared straight ahead. She was afraid to look at Joel. She didn't want him to think she was waiting for him to ask her to dance.

Think of something to say, she told herself. *Something funny.* The harder she tried to think, the more her mind stayed blank. The loud music seemed to mingle with the sound of blood rushing in her ears.

She was concentrating so hard she almost didn't notice when Joel turned to her and said something.

Sophie leaned in closer. "What?" she shouted over the music.

At that moment, the doors near them banged open. Joel and Sophie turned. Keisha and Courtney strode into the room, with the rest of the cheerleaders in tow. They were all dressed like cowgirls in cutoff jeans or denim skirts, plaid shirts, and boots. Written across the crowns of their cowboy hats were the words MULE DRIVERS.

Sophie stared. They had obviously gotten dressed together. So there had been a party at Courtney's after all. And she hadn't been invited. Sophie felt a pit in the bottom of her stomach.

Just then, Keisha spotted her. She swooped over and slung her arm around Sophie's neck. "Hi, Itsy-Bitsy!" she hollered. "Come join the group."

Before Sophie could say anything to Joel, Keisha pulled her away.

"Hey, Sophie!" the other cheerleaders said when they saw her.

Courtney folded her arms. She looked at Sophie from under lashes heavy with mascara. "What are you? The Jolly Green Midget?"

"I'm, um, a green M&M."

"You're so cute, Bitsy," said Keisha.

"So, you guys all got dressed together?" Sophie tried to sound casual.

"Yeah, we were over at Courtney's house," Keisha told her. "I wondered why you weren't there."

"Nobody . . . I mean, I wasn't . . . I didn't know if I should come."

"Oh?" Keisha raised her eyebrows. She turned and looked at Courtney. "Courtney didn't tell you?"

Courtney's smile reminded Sophie of a crocodile's. "I guess I forgot to mention it," she said with a shrug.

Keisha put her arm around Sophie. "Our bad, Bitsy."

She sounded genuinely sorry. Sophie looked around at the other cheerleaders. Amy and Angie gave her sympathetic looks. Maybe Courtney had really forgotten to mention it to her, Sophie thought. Maybe it had just been a mistake.

The slow song ended, and a fast one came on.

"Come on!" Keisha said. "Let's dance!" With her

arm still around Sophie's shoulders, she headed for the dance floor, dragging Sophie along.

For a second, Sophie caught a glimpse of Joel watching her. She tried to give him an apologetic look, but the rest of the cheerleaders surged around, blocking her view. They put their arms around each other's shoulders, forming a big circle.

The cheerleaders danced that way for several songs. They jumped up and down and sang along to the music. Sophie could feel the envious looks from other kids in the gym. She was certain they wished they could be on the inside of the circle, too.

After a while, another slow song came on. The circle broke up. A few football players who had been standing nearby asked some of the girls to dance. Joy, Amy, and the twins wandered out into the hall to get a drink of water. Sophie decided to look for Kylie and Joel.

She had just started to circle the cafeteria when she ran into Scott. He was wearing a sombrero and a Mexican-style poncho.

"Hey, Sophie," he said. "You're here. So, what are you?"

Sophie sighed. "A green M&M," she said unenthusiastically.

Scott laughed. "That's cool."

"What are you?"

Scott shrugged. "Uh, a guy in a sombrero? I don't know. I just found this stuff in my older brother's room. I'm not really into making costumes."

"Me, neither," said Sophie.

"So, do you want to dance?"

"Okay."

They moved onto the dance floor. Scott put his hands on Sophie's waist, and she put her hands on his shoulders. They shifted from foot to foot, revolving in time to the music.

This wasn't the first time Sophie had danced with a boy, but it was the first time she'd danced with someone as tall as Scott. She found herself staring at the middle of his chest. When he exhaled she could feel his breath on the top of her head.

Here was Sophie Smith, former nobody, dancing with the most popular guy in school. *This should be the highlight of my year*, Sophie thought. But even as she danced with Scott, she found herself thinking about Joel. Scott was cute and sweet, but, well, there here was no one like Joel Leo.

But what if Joel was dancing with someone else? The thought made her stomach drop. Sophie began to surreptitiously scan the room. Before long she spotted Joel on the other side of the cafeteria. He was with Kylie, and they weren't dancing. They were both watching Sophie.

Kylie looked stunned.

She thinks I'm with Scott! Sophie thought. Sophie tried to signal with her eyes that Kylie had misunderstood. But before she could, Scott turned her, continuing his slow revolution. Sophie looked back over her shoulder at Kylie. Instead, she found herself locking eyes with Courtney. Courtney smiled in a way that sent chills down Sophie's spine.

To Sophie's relief, the song ended. Scott and Sophie moved apart. "Thanks," he said.

"Thanks," echoed Sophie distractedly. She looked around for Courtney again and saw her talking to Keisha. As she watched, both girls glanced in Sophie's direction.

Suddenly, Sophie was more anxious than ever to find Kylie. She wanted to explain that she and Scott were just friends, just in case Kylie had misunderstood. She circled the cafeteria once, scanning the crowd. She circled again. By the third loop she realized that Kylie and Joel were gone.

Sophie made her way back over to the cheerleaders. They were dancing in a circle again, arms tightly woven around one another's shoulders. Sophie bounced around outside the group for a while, waiting for them to let her in. But no one

127

seemed to notice her. Eventually, she gave up and moved over to the wall to watch.

All over the cafeteria, groups of kids were dancing together in little knots. Sophie didn't know any of them well enough to join them. She hoped maybe Kylie and Joel had just gone outside to get some air. After half an hour, though, she had to admit that they weren't coming back.

With a sigh, Sophie dug some change out of her pocket, went to the pay phone in the hall, and called her mother to come pick her up.

CHAPTER
Twelve

Kylie wasn't speaking to Sophie.

When Sophie called Kylie's house on Saturday, Mrs. Lovett said that Kylie wasn't home. But Sophie was almost sure she'd heard Kylie's voice in the background. She'd called again Saturday afternoon and again on Sunday. By Sunday night it was clear that Kylie wasn't calling back.

Sophie didn't know why Kylie wasn't talking to her. On Monday, she caught her at her locker and confronted her. Kylie had just swished her hair and said, "Why don't you ask your cheerleader friends?"

Sophie couldn't ask her cheerleader friends, though, because they weren't talking to her, either. That Monday at practice, when Sophie asked a question about a cheer, Keisha turned to Courtney

129

and said, "Do you hear something?" Sophie repeated her question, but no one would answer, or even look at her. For the rest of the day, whenever Sophie tried to speak, Keisha or Courtney starting talking over her, as if Sophie were nothing more than an annoying fly buzzing in the background.

The twins caught on. By Tuesday, Sophie couldn't so much as say hello without them laughing hysterically. The other cheerleaders wouldn't speak to her either. Kate and Trisha snubbed her in the halls. Amy, Angie, and Joy wouldn't make room for her at their table at lunch. When they couldn't avoid her, they ignored her.

On Wednesday, Sophie cornered Angie in the bathroom and asked her what was going on.

"Well, I'm not completely sure," said Angie, watching the door as if she feared Keisha might walk in any minute. "But the twins told Amy that they heard Courtney telling Keisha that you were all over Scott at the dance. Scott is Keisha's ex-boyfriend, you know. They went out for three weeks last year."

"I didn't know that," Sophie told her. "But I wasn't hanging on Scott. I swear I don't even like him!" Angie just shrugged and edged out the bathroom door. Sophie wondered why Kate hadn't stuck up for her. Kate knew that Sophie didn't like

Scott — Sophie had told her in the note in math class. So why was Kate being mean to her now?

And was that why Kylie was mad, too? Because she thought Sophie liked Scott?

Sophie would have liked to ask someone these questions, but there was no one to ask. Not Joel, who hadn't so much as looked at her since the night of the dance. Not Amy or Angie, who hadn't spoken to her in over a week. Their awe of Keisha seemed to outweigh their natural instinct to be friendly. After Sophie's interrogation in the bathroom, they had gone out of their way to avoid her.

Not even her parents had much to say to Sophie these days. They'd had a *lot* to say when they received the latest credit card bill, which arrived the Monday after the dance. Her father, red in the face, had delivered a very loud lecture about responsibility and bad spending habits. Her mother, who seemed mostly alarmed by how much Sophie had spent on mascara, chimed in with a few teary comments about broken trust. Their speech was so long that at the end of it her parents, unaccustomed to giving lectures, had looked as exhausted and miserable as Sophie felt. But after they'd taken away her credit card and phone privileges, they'd settled into a stony silence that made Sophie almost wish they'd go back to scolding her.

On the bright side, Sophie told herself (since there was no one else to tell), at least being grounded wasn't so bad. She didn't have anyone to hang out with, anyway.

The only person who was talking to Sophie was Scott. Every day at their lockers he greeted her with a cheerful "Hey, Sophie," seemingly oblivious to the drama that was swirling around them. And Sophie, determined not to lose what seemed to be her one friend left in the world, returned his greeting and tried to ignore the poisonous looks from any of Keisha's friends who happened to overhear.

One day, Sophie rounded a corner and almost ran into Kylie. Sophie was wearing the dragon jeans that day. Kylie, it turned out, was wearing them, too. For a moment the two girls stared at each other.

"Kye —" Sophie began.

But before she could say more, Kylie turned on her heel. When Sophie saw her later that day, Kylie had changed into the track pants she usually wore to practice.

Kylie wasn't just mad, Sophie realized with a shock. She didn't want to have anything to do with Sophie.

After two weeks of the silent treatment, Sophie felt ready to snap. Tears seemed to be constantly on the verge of spilling from her eyes. Then one day at cheerleading practice Sophie fell out of a lift and hit the ground hard, and finally the tears came.

Ms. Charge stood over Sophie, her hands on her hips, frowning with concern. "Are you hurt?" she barked.

Sophie shook her head. She was crying too hard to say anything.

"Stand up and walk it off."

Sophie wobbled to her feet, still crying.

Ms. Charge regarded her for a second. "Take a lap around the field," she told Sophie. Then she added more gently, "Walk, don't run. Just take a breather."

All the other girls were watching. Sophie heard Keisha and Courtney snicker as she set off to walk around the perimeter of the football field. "Stop crying," she whispered to herself angrily. But the tears had been building for days, and they just kept coming.

She had finally managed to get them under control when she heard feet pounding the ground behind her.

"Are you okay?"

It was Alyssa. She slowed to a walk next to Sophie.

Sophie nodded.

"I'm sorry I didn't catch you."

"It's not your fault." And it hadn't been Alyssa's fault. They had been practicing a shoulder stand. Sophie was supposed to stand with her feet on Angie's shoulders. For the stunt to work, Sophie had to keep her legs locked and her muscles tight. But Sophie had let go too soon and tumbled forward. There was no way Alyssa, who was standing behind, could have caught her.

They walked in silence for a moment.

"So, what's up?" said Alyssa.

Sophie snuffled. "What do you mean?"

"The pep assembly is next week. All the other groups on the team have their shoulder stand down. But you haven't managed to hit it yet."

The shoulder stands were going to be the finale of the cheerleaders' big routine at the pep assembly. All three flyers had to be in the shoulder stands. If Sophie couldn't get the stand down, the formation would be ruined.

"You've always been really good at stunts," Alyssa told Sophie. "But lately it's like your mind is in outer space."

Sophie's throat ached. She was so grateful to have someone talking to her, she was afraid she might start crying again.

But this time instead of tears, words came spilling out. Sophie told Alyssa about Keisha and Courtney's campaign against her, how none of the other cheerleaders would talk to her.

"You can't let those girls get to you," Alyssa told her.

"It's kind of hard not to."

"Let me tell you something about Keisha," said Alyssa. "She's a good cheerleader, and I respect that. But the only person she cares about is herself. She'll act like your best friend one minute, then she'll drop you like a dirty Kleenex the next, just so you'll fall all over yourself trying to get her to like you again. Haven't you ever noticed how she leads the twins around by their noses?"

Sophie nodded.

"She does it to everyone," said Alyssa. "She even tries to do it to me. I just don't go along with her."

"What about Courtney?" asked Sophie.

Alyssa snorted. "Courtney's just plain mean. I think she's always worried that Keisha is going to drop her and she takes it out on everyone else. Plus, she hates anybody she thinks is prettier than she is."

"But Courtney's pretty," Sophie pointed out.

"She's not, really. She just wears a lot of makeup. That doesn't necessarily make you pretty."

Sophie thought about that. Suddenly, she felt stupid for spending seventeen dollars on mascara. "So, you're saying that's why they turned everyone against me?" She asked Alyssa. "'Cause Courtney is jealous and Keisha is just being Keisha?"

"It might be," said Alyssa. "It probably doesn't help that you're friends with Kylie."

"*Was* friends," Sophie corrected her.

"Really?" Alyssa looked at her. "That's too bad. I think Kylie's pretty cool. I thought it was rotten what Keisha and Courtney did to her at the Halloween dance. Wearing those mule-driver outfits just to burn her."

Sophie was startled. She hadn't even thought about what mule driver meant. She'd been too worried about the fact that they hadn't invited her to get dressed with them. No wonder Kylie had been upset.

"It drives Keisha crazy when Kylie shows her up at the games. Keisha can't stand anyone upstaging her." Alyssa chuckled. "It's kind of funny watching her face, actually."

They had almost circled back around to the cheerleaders. Sophie stopped. Alyssa stopped, too.

"So, why do you do it?" Sophie asked.

"What? Why do I cheer?" Alyssa paused. "I do it 'cause I like it. All this stuff —" Alyssa flapped her hands to indicate everything they'd been talking about — "is not cheerleading." She pointed to the girls, who were still practicing shoulder stands. "*That* is cheerleading. So are you ready to cheer, or what?"

Sophie swallowed and looked over at the other girls. Slowly, she nodded.

Alyssa grinned. "Well, then. Come on!"

The more Sophie thought about what Alyssa had said, the more she felt she owed Kylie an apology. The problem was how to do it.

Sophie went through all the options. She couldn't call Kylie and say she was sorry, since she had lost her phone privileges. She couldn't talk to her at school — Kylie walked the other way whenever she saw Sophie coming. She could go over to Kylie's house, but she was afraid Mr. or Mrs. Lovett would be there, and Sophie didn't want to make a scene.

At last she decided to write Kylie a note. It took her all weekend to do it, and she went through four sheets of paper. In the end, the note read:

Stylie Kylie,

I know you're mad at me right now, and although I don't exactly know all the reasons why, you have sure given me plenty of time to think about it. The more I think about it, the more I realize I have put a lot more time into cheerleading than I have into our friendship lately. I am sorry for that. I guess I got a little carried away with all the excitement, but now I know that some of that excitement is nothing more than a bunch of drama. Also, maybe you think I like Scott Hersh, but I don't. We're just friends. But just so you know, he's not a dumb jock.

I miss you, Kylie. I hope we can still be friends.

Your friend forever,

Sophie

Now Sophie had to figure out how to give it to her. She was afraid if she handed it to Kylie, she would throw it out without even reading it. The best thing to do, she decided, was to put it in Kylie's locker.

But she never got the chance. On Monday, just as she was about to slip the note in Kylie's locker, Scott happened to pass by. He stopped to chat. When Kylie saw Sophie and Scott talking in front of *her* locker, she gave Sophie such a look of cold fury that Sophie was afraid to even pass by Kylie's locker for two whole days.

On Thursday, she worked up the nerve to try again. As she turned down the hall to Kylie's locker, she saw Kylie talking with Joel. Sophie could've sworn she heard Kylie say her name. Sophie slunk past them, the note still in her pocket.

At last, Sophie decided to wait and give Kylie the note on Friday. The pep rally was Friday morning, and she would put the note in Kylie's locker Friday afternoon, right after the rally.

Friday morning every seat in the gymnasium was filled. The whole school was crammed into the bleachers — sixth-, seventh-, and eighth-graders. In the center of the gym, the student council performed a skit dressed as Vikings, the Northwest mascot. Meridian's second big game against Northwest was that afternoon, which was the reason for the pep assembly. Whoever won this game would go on to the district championship.

Sophie and the other cheerleaders stood on the sidelines, waiting to go on. Sophie had no idea what the student council skit was about. She was too excited and nervous to pay attention. Now was the big moment. For once, they wouldn't be cheering from the sidelines. They'd be the main attraction.

Unlike the short cheers they usually did at the games, their routine was a dance to an entire song and involved lots of stunts. At one point, Sophie and Amy, the two best tumblers on the team, did backflips. All the flyers did basket tosses, where they were thrown in the air and caught in the hands of the other girls. And then there was the shoulder stand at the end of the dance.

As soon as they hit their final formation, Kylie was supposed to run on and do her Mules Rules. Over the past few games, the Rules had become very popular. Kylie no longer even had to hold up the written signs. She'd just hold up a number and everyone would shout the corresponding rule.

The more success Kylie had with the crowd, the more frustrated Keisha became. Ever since the crowd started reacting to the mascot, the tension between Keisha and Kylie had thickened, until they could barely be in a room together. Now that Kylie wasn't talking to Sophie, she barely communicated with the squad. But on the field, you never would have known it. And the fans still adored her.

At last, the skit ended. When the audience had

finished clapping, Keisha gave them the signal. The cheerleaders took the floor, doing cartwheels and back handsprings.

They had just started the dance when Sophie realized something was wrong. There was another sound playing over the top of their music. At first she couldn't tell what it was. Then she heard it.

HEE-HAW! HEE-HAW!

Sounds of a mule braying blared from a boom box set up at the side of the gym.

Kylie, wearing her mule suit, was running up and down the bleachers, in between all the assembled kids. As she ran, she threw handfuls of hay at the crowd.

The cheerleaders continued with their dance, but no one was watching them. All eyes were on Kylie. When she ran out of hay, she loped to the middle of the gym and stood in front of the cheerleaders.

She held up a poster board sign. She was starting the Mules Rules early.

Only Sophie realized they weren't the Mules Rules, not exactly. The kids in the gymnasium hollered out the signs as she held them over her head.

"BE COOL!

OVERRULE!

DON'T CHEER
FOR *THOSE* FOOLS!"

Kylie dropped the sign, turned, and pointed at the cheerleaders.

For a moment, Sophie wasn't sure what was going on. The other cheerleaders had all stopped dancing. The entire gymnasium was in an uproar. Lots of kids were laughing. Others were yelling "Boooo!"

Sophie looked over and saw Keisha shouting something at Kylie. She was so angry, the veins in her temples were standing out. But Sophie couldn't hear what she was saying over the noises. She looked in the other direction and saw Ms. Charge. Her mouth hung open in a perfect O.

Then she understood. Kylie had burned them. She'd burned all the cheerleaders right in front of the entire school.

In the middle of the gym, Kylie danced as if she'd scored a touchdown, which just made the kids in the bleachers holler louder. Sophie could no longer even hear their dance music over all the noise.

The principal took the microphone and threatened to send everyone back to class if they didn't calm down.

Sophie didn't stick around to find out if they

calmed down. She ran from the gym straight to her locker. As soon as she got there, she tore up the note. Kylie had humiliated the whole cheerleading team. Nothing in the world would make Sophie apologize to her now!

CHAPTER
Thirteen

On Friday afternoon, Ms. Charge called an emergency meeting of the pep squad, which meant all the cheerleaders, plus Kylie. She paced up and down in front of them, hands clasped behind her back, brow furrowed like a judge. Today her T-shirt read, ATHLETES LIFT WEIGHTS, CHEERLEADERS LIFT ATHLETES, but Ms. Charge looked like she wanted to lift Kylie and throw her out the window.

First, she'd wanted to know if anyone had helped Kylie plan her cheerleader ambush. Kylie, sitting apart from the rest of the team, calmly said no, she'd thought of it all herself. Sophie had to admit Kylie had guts. The most popular girls in school were sitting three feet away staring daggers at her, and Kylie acted like she didn't have a care in the world.

After another lengthy speech about teamwork, during which even Keisha, who'd been gloating throughout the entire scene, started to wilt, Ms. Charge asked the cheerleaders what they thought should be done. "Suspend her," Keisha said at once. "Make sure she can't cheer at the games any more."

Ms. Charge raised her eyebrows. She looked around at the other cheerleaders. "Does everyone agree that Kylie should be suspended?"

The other cheerleaders nodded. A few said, "Yeah."

Sophie glanced at Kylie. She didn't want to see her suspended from the squad. But she couldn't bring herself to stand up for Kylie either. After all, Kylie certainly didn't seem to be on Sophie's side.

Sophie sat there, frozen with undecision, until it was too late to say anything.

"All right," said Ms. Charge. "It's the team's decision that Kylie should be suspended.

"That means," Ms. Charge turned to Kylie, "you cannot mascot at the game this afternoon — or any other game until the team feels you're ready to join again."

Kylie just shrugged.

Angie raised her hand. "But who will be the mascot?"

"We don't need a mascot, Angie," Keisha snapped, giving her a withering look.

But for once Keisha was overruled. The other cheerleaders agreed that, in fact, they *did* need a mascot. Northwest's mascot would surely be at the game. If the Mule wasn't there, it would look like Meridian didn't have spirit.

Several ideas for Kylie's replacement were thrown out. Angie suggested Mr. Green, the vice principal, who was a gangly, goofy man, but they quickly realized the costume wouldn't fit him. Courtney suggested calling last year's mascot, but no one could remember his name. Joy suggested Ms. Charge, and everyone, including Ms. Charge, looked at her like she was crazy. During the entire conversation, Kylie studied her nails and didn't say a word.

Finally, they decided they would ask Howard Heller. Howard was the cymbals player in the school band, the one who was always bashing the cymbals together at the wrong moment. All the cheerleaders agreed that this was a good solution. Not only would they have a mascot, but without Howard playing, the quality of the school band would be significantly improved.

That afternoon after school, Keisha and Courtney cornered Howard and told him he was going to be the mascot. Howard was so astonished that Keisha was talking to him, he would have agreed to anything she said.

At last, it was time for the game to start. As the teams lined up for the kickoff, the tension in the bleachers was thick.

For the first quarter, the score remained tied. The cheerleaders did cheer after cheer. Sophie yelled until she started to feel hoarse.

Howard, wearing the Mule mascot costume, lumbered up and down the sidelines. Occasionally, he would raise one arm and shake his fist, like someone who had just discovered he had been cheated and was vowing to get back at the person who did it.

"He's awful!" Amy said to Sophie as they watched Howard between cheers.

In the second quarter, Meridian started to fall behind.

Keisha called the pep team into a huddle. "We need to keep everyone's spirit up," she instructed. "Howard, do a wave."

When the huddle broke, Howard dutifully trotted back to the sidelines. He ran up and down in front of the bleachers, trying to get the crowd to do a wave. But at that exact moment, the Meridian kicker was lining up for a field goal. All eyes were on the game. Nobody was looking at Howard.

The kicker booted the ball. It swerved left. Everyone groaned. No one did the wave.

"He's worse at being a mascot than he is at playing cymbals," Angie said to Sophie.

Just then a shout went up from the other side of the field. The Northwest cheerleaders had all turned to face Meridian.

"We've got spirit, yes, we do!" the Northwest cheerleaders and fans shouted. "We've got spirit, how 'bout you?"

They were starting a spirit war. Sophie and the rest of the cheerleaders had no choice but to try to rally the Meridian fans.

"We've got spirit, yes, we do! We've got spirit, how 'bout you?" They yelled their loudest, but they couldn't make up for the listless crowd.

"We've got spirit, we've got more! If you don't believe us, just look at the score!" The Northwest cheerleaders swiveled and pointed to the scoreboard.

Northwest was leading by fourteen points. Meridian was losing the game, and the Meridian cheerleaders had no response. How could they get the crowd energized when they felt defeated themselves?

Keisha called another huddle. "We need to do an offense cheer," she told the cheerleaders.

"What we need is *Kylie*!" cried Sophie. The words were out of her mouth before she'd even realized she was going to say them.

Everyone turned to stare at her. "We do *not* need Kylie," said Keisha, giving Sophie a murderous look.

"Yes, we do!" Sophie couldn't believe she was standing up to Keisha, but she was. Her heart beat faster with a mixture of fear and elation. She knew what was right, and she'd finally found the nerve to say it. "We need her, and we need the Mules Rules. That's the only thing that will get the crowd's spirit back up."

"But Kylie is suspended," Amy said, wide-eyed. "She can't cheer at the game."

Sophie replied, "Amy, remember after the last game with Northwest? You said Kylie's cheering rallied the team. You were right. We were behind by fifteen points —"

"Seventeen," corrected Kate, who always kept track of the scores.

"We were behind by *seventeen* points," Sophie amended. "And when Kylie came on the field the fans got psyched up and the team came back."

Around the circle, heads began to nod — Renee, Amy, Angie, Joy, even the twins agreed. They all remembered the effect the Mules Rules had had at that game.

"I can't believe you guys are even considering this," said Keisha, "after what she did to us at the pep rally."

The girls stopped nodding. Keisha had a point.

"That was messed up," Sophie agreed. "And I'm mad at her, too. But you have to admit she has a way with the crowd."

Alyssa suddenly spoke up. "I think we can consider this a cheer emergency. You know, drastic times call for drastic measures." She gave Sophie a smile. Sophie grinned, relieved to have someone back her up.

Keisha looked around furiously. She could sense she was losing control. "Well, what will Ms. Charge say?"

"Let's ask her!" Sophie cried. She turned to go get Ms. Charge. But she didn't have to. The coach was already charging down the sidelines toward them.

"Why are you all standing around?" she demanded. "The team's drowning out there! The *fans* are drowning."

"Ms. Charge," Alyssa said somberly, "we believe this is a cheer emergency. We'd like to bring Kylie back."

"Howard's not cutting it," Joy added bluntly.

Ms. Charge glanced over at Howard. He was trying to do the tail shake, but he looked like he was doubled over with gas pains. "He's terrible," she agreed. She turned back to the team. "Is this what you all want?" she asked.

"No!" said Keisha. "It's not what we *all* want."

Ms. Charge folded her arms. "I may act like a dictator," she said, "but I can run a democracy. Let's vote. All those who want Kylie back on the field — just for this game — put your hands up."

Sophie raised her hand. So did Alyssa, Renee, Joy, Amy, and Angie. Keisha, Courtney, Trisha, and Kate kept their hands down. The twins glanced at Keisha and tentatively raised their hands. She scowled. Quickly, they lowered them again.

It was tied, six and six. Then, to Sophie's astonishment, Kate's hand crept into the air.

"Kate!" Keisha and Courtney shrieked in outrage.

"What?" said Kate. She tossed her hair. "I think it's a good idea."

"That's it, then. We bring Kylie back," said Ms. Charge.

"But I'm head cheerleader," Keisha burst out. "Shouldn't my vote count twice?"

Ms. Charge gave her a tired look. "Keisha, your mouth might be big enough for two people. But you only get one vote."

Keisha's mouth fell open. Sophie hid her smile behind her hand.

"Now that we've got that solved," said Ms. Charge, "does anyone know if Kylie is even here?"

"I'll bet she is!" said Sophie. She broke away from the group and began to run along the foot of the bleachers, scanning the crowd.

She saw Joel first. Kylie was sitting right next to him. She wore dark glasses and a hat, her golden curls cascading down around her shoulders, as conspicuously inconspicuous as she possibly could be.

Sophie took the steps two at a time. "Sorry, Joel," she said when she reached them. "I have to borrow Kylie for a minute."

Before Kylie could protest, Sophie grabbed her wrist and dragged her down the stairs.

"We need you," Sophie said when they were standing to the side of the bleachers. "You have to do the Mules Rules."

"I can't," Kylie said coolly. "I'm suspended, remember?"

"Ms. Charge said you can come back for this game." Sophie pointed to the sidelines, where Ms. Charge and the rest of the team were watching them.

"Well, maybe I don't want to," said Kylie. "I'm not exactly welcome out there."

"We voted," Sophie told her. "Almost everyone wants you to come back. The team is losing. The crowd is fading. We need someone to get the spirit back up. And Howard is not the one."

"He's the worst," agreed Kylie.

"So, will you do it? Please?" Sophie paused, then added, "I'll be your best friend."

Kylie looked at Sophie for a long moment. "Okay," she said at last.

Quickly, they located Howard. Sophie told him to take off the suit and give it to Kylie. Howard didn't mind. He was just glad to have cheerleaders paying attention to him.

As soon as Kylie was on the field, Alyssa said, "We're running out of time. We need to do the Mules Rules now, before the second half."

Kylie mumbled something from inside the mask.

"What?" said Alyssa.

Kylie repeated it.

"She said she doesn't have her signs with numbers on them," said Amy, who was standing closest to her. "So, she doesn't have any way to signal the crowd."

Sophie smiled. "I have an idea," she said.

A moment later, the cheerleaders and Kylie were back out in front of the crowd. The cheerleaders waved their pom-poms and kicked their legs high in the air.

Kylie kicked her legs, too. She did her goofy cartwheels. She danced around. She did everything she could to let the fans know she was back.

They noticed. The crowd seemed to perk up a little. "Go, Mules!" a few people shouted.

The cheerleaders got into position. "MULES RULES!" they shouted in unison.

Behind Sophie, Alyssa quietly counted, "One, two, hit!" A second later, Sophie was standing straight and tall on Angie's shoulders.

Next to her, Keisha was on Courtney's shoulders. And to the other side of Keisha, Renee stood on Amie's shoulders. They were finally getting a chance to do their shoulder stands. And everyone had hit them perfectly.

High in the air, Sophie and Renee raised their right arms in a number one sign.

In the center, Keisha kept her hands on her hips and her lips pressed tight together. She was boycotting the Mules Rules. But it didn't matter. The crowd got it, anyway.

"RULE NUMBER ONE!" the cheerleaders yelled.

"HAVE FUN!" the crowd yelled back.

"RULE NUMBER TWO!" called the cheerleaders.

"DON'T DROOL!" the crowd responded. A few people whistled. On the ground in front of the cheerleaders, Kylie danced like crazy.

"RULE NUMBER THREE!"

"CHEER LIKE FOOLS FOR YOUR SCHOOL! CUZ THE MULES . . . RULE!"

Right before "Rule!" the flyers all dropped and were caught by their spotters. All the girls raised their arms in a V for Victory sign. Kylie bucked her feet in the air. The crowd whooped and hollered.

For the second half of the game, Kylie cheered right alongside the cheerleaders, acting goofier than ever.

Meridian came back. In the end, they won, 31–28.

As players trotted off the field, the cheerleaders lifted Kylie onto their shoulders. The band played an off-key version of "We Are the Champions." Howard was back on cymbals, blissfully bashing them together at all the wrong moments.

Sophie grinned. Everything was as it should be. Kylie was a mule. Howard was a cymbals player. The eighth-grade football team would go on to the district championships.

And she finally had her proof that the cheering made a difference.

Later that afternoon, Sophie and Kylie walked down the school's main hallway. Kylie was still wearing the fuzzy brown mule suit, though she was carrying the mask.

"Thanks for coming through," Sophie told Kylie.

"It was actually fun," she replied. "I guess I'm better at being a mule than I ever wanted to be."

They stopped in front of the counselor's office. "Well," said Kylie, "this is where I get off." Ms. Charge had said she wanted to meet with Kylie in the counselor's office.

"I'll wait for you here," Sophie told her.

"You don't have to."

"I know that. I want to."

Kylie smiled. "Well, here goes." She took a deep breath and walked into the office.

Suddenly, Sophie felt exhausted. She leaned against the wall and let her body slide down until she was sitting on the floor. Today felt like the longest day of her life.

Still, it had all been worth it. And it *definitely* had been worth it to see Keisha's face when Kylie was lifted into the air, Sophie thought. She knew now why Alyssa enjoyed it so much.

She wondered what Ms. Charge and the counselor were saying to Kylie on the other side of the door. Considering that Ms. Charge was in there, it was strangely quiet.

A door to the outside opened at the end of the hallway, and a figure appeared, silhouetted against the daylight. As it came closer, Sophie saw that it was Joel.

"Hi," she said as he walked up to the office.

"Hey," Joel replied. He seemed surprised to see her sitting on the floor. "I was just looking for Kylie. The other girls said she'd be here."

"She's inside," Sophie told him. She sounded calmer than she felt. It was the first time she and Joel had spoken since the Halloween dance, and her insides were jumping like grasshoppers.

Joel nodded. "So . . . good game."

Sophie smiled. "Yeah, Kylie was good."

"You were all good," Joel said quickly. He brushed a lock of hair back behind his ear. "I mean, you looked really good, too. Those stunts and everything."

"Thanks." Sophie blushed.

"Do you want to wait for Kylie with me?" she asked.

"Nah," said Joel. "I have to get home. But I'll see you around?"

"Okay," said Sophie. She watched him as he walked back down the hall.

Finally, the office door opened. Kylie came out.

"Well?" said Sophie.

Kylie sat down next to her. She hesitated a moment, then said, "I'm finished."

"No!" said Sophie. "That is so unfair. You saved

the game today! Maybe we can get a petition together. We can get the cheerleaders to sign it. And the football players, and —"

"Wait." Kylie held up a hand. "It's okay. Ms. Charge told me I could stay on the team. But I quit."

Sophie stared at her. "Why?"

Kylie shrugged. "I don't know. It's like Ms. Charge said. I'm not really a team player."

It's true, Sophie thought. *Kylie definitely marches to the beat of her own drum.*

"But what about the Mules Rules?" Sophie asked. "You made them up. They're yours."

"They don't need me just for the Mules Rules. Someone else can do them."

"But no one will do them as well as you."

Kylie nodded. "That's true."

Sophie looked at Kylie's fuzzy brown suit. "I'm going to miss you in that outfit," she said.

"Me, too," said Kylie. *"Not!"*

They both laughed. Then their chuckles faded into silence. They sat quietly for a moment. Sophie knew what she had to say.

But Kylie spoke first. "I'm sorry about dissing you guys at the pep assembly. I guess that wasn't very cool. Some of those girls are okay."

"Yeah, some of them are," agreed Sophie. "And some of them aren't. I'm sorry about what happened at the Halloween dance. About ditching you to hang out with the cheerleaders, I mean."

"That was pretty lousy," Kylie admitted. "I mostly felt bad for Joel, though."

"For Joel?"

"When you wouldn't dance with him."

Sophie frowned, confused. "I would have danced with him if he'd asked me."

"He *did* ask you, but you walked away."

Sophie's mind whirled. She remembered Joel turning to her to say something just as the cheerleaders walked in. Joel had wanted to dance. With her.

"I shouldn't tell you this," Kylie confessed, "but he likes you. Or he did, anyway."

"I thought he liked *you*," said Sophie, dumbfounded. "I mean, you've been hanging out all the time, so I thought you guys . . ."

"What? Me and Joel?" Kylie squawked. "Ew! No way."

"Do you think . . . he might like me again?" Sophie asked hesitantly.

Kylie smiled. "Maybe. That is, if he can get over you being a cheerleader."

Sophie turned pink all the way to her ear tips.

"But what about you and Scott?" said Kylie. "'Cause I've been hearing rumors —"

"None of which are true," Sophie said quickly. "I've been trying to tell you, we're just friends. I would never step in on someone you like. Or even *used* to like."

"I guess I still like him. I don't think he'll ever get over that attack by his locker though."

"You never know," said Sophie.

"Hmm," said Kylie, thinking about that. She turned her back to Sophie. "I think I'm ready to get out of this costume. Would you unzip me?"

Sophie undid the zipper and Kylie wriggled out of the furry suit.

She held it up. "What should I do with it?"

"Turn it into a fur coat?" suggested Sophie.

"It would make a nice rug," said Kylie.

"Or boots!"

"How about a fabulous set of furry pom-poms?" Kylie joked. "I can wave them at the games. You can show me some cool moves."

Sophie shook her head. "Sorry. Can't do it. I'm sworn to cheerleader secrecy."

"C'mon." Kylie poked her in the side. "Give 'em up. I'll be your best friend."

Sophie swatted away her hand. Then she put an arm around Kylie's shoulders.

"Okay," she said, laughing. "It's a deal."

check out

THE BOY
NEXT DOOR

Another

candy Apple book . . .

just for you.

candy
Apple

Chapter 1

❀❀❀ TARYN ❀❀❀

I Guess It's a Boy Thing

"Jeff Rasmussen, I'm going to get you for this!" I scream at the top of my lungs.

My head pounds and I reach up to make sure there's no bump. Meanwhile, Jeff zips across my lawn into his own backyard, taunting me the whole time.

"You can run," I scream even louder, "but you can't hide!"

I can't believe Jeff would do this. Sure, he's been teasing me for eleven summers straight. There have been times over the years when he's even dared to pinch or poke me, but he usually keeps his distance. And he never actually *hit* me with anything before, especially not a flying object. Mostly he just calls me obnoxious names like "stinky" and "bones. " He sure knows how to make me squirm, the rat.

Of course, I've plotted my own kind of revenge. It drives Jeff crazy when I tease him right back about the two extra-long toes on his left foot. And I got him once with a mean triple-knuckled noogie. The main difference between my teasing and his, however, are the aftershocks.

A single harsh word from Jeff and I'm bawling for five minutes.

But Jeff's different. He never ever cries. He just laughs out loud.

I guess it's a boy thing.

Jeff's family and my family have been friends forever. His mom and my mom always remind us that Jeff and I were born on the exact same week-end at the same hospital in Rochester, New York. We both weighed exactly seven pounds and four ounces, and measured twenty inches. Sometimes I wonder if Jeff is actually my secret twin brother, except that I don't really need (or want) another brother. I already have three of those: Tim, Tom, and Todd. Three Taylor brothers is more than enough for anyone.

I guess the worst part about Jeff's sneak attack

today was that he didn't hit me with a Wiffle ball or anything accidental. No, he hit me with a sneaker aimed directly at my head — a smelly, brown, disgusting sneaker with a rubber sole that's peeling off.

How gross is that?

"Jeff, where are you?" I growl, climbing over the break in the fence between our houses. I scramble through the thicket, trying hard not to scratch up my legs. I'm already covered from head to toe with mosquito bites.

It's too warm out today. The air feels like mashed potatoes and I can't find Jeff anywhere. He's not in the small shed behind his house. He's not under his front porch. I've checked all of his usual hiding spots.

I'm getting thirsty.

"Jeff, come out!" I cry. "Come on, it's too hot. Truce? Please?"

Jeff appears from around the side of his blue-shingled house. He's whistling and carrying two Popsicles. I take a cherry one. He keeps the lime. We sit on the porch steps. I realize that he's still only wearing one sneaker, the one he didn't hurl at my head.

"That really, really hurt, you know," I grumble, biting the end of my Popsicle.

He looks right through me. "Yeah, sorry, Taryn," he says. I want to believe him, but he's smirking.

"You're sorry?" I repeat, my eyes widening.

"Yeah, sorry. Truly."

"You mean it?" I ask, twisting the ends of my long, brown hair.

"Yeah," Jeff replies. "I didn't really mean to hit you. I just got carried away. And I know how gross my sneakers are."

He sounds genuine this time. As if.

But somehow, despite all the teasing over the years, Jeff always finds the right thing to say or do to make things better. Somehow, a word or even just a smile is like a Band-Aid, and I can instantly forgive Jeff for whatever he's done.

That's how it works with best friends.

Jeff leaves me on the porch with his Popsicle peace offering and races across the lawn, back to my yard. He's gone to find his other stinky shoe. He returns with both sneakers laced up and a yellow dandelion tight in his fist.

"Here," Jeff grunts, pushing the little flower toward me.

Now it's my turn to laugh. "Thanks," I say with a smile, taking the flower. It's peace offering number two. I'm secretly glad that he's feeling so guilty.

The sun beats down hard on the steps, so we

move up to the wicker rocking chairs on his porch. We've spent more afternoons than I can count rocking in those chairs together. Sometimes we play Scrabble or cards out there. Sometimes his mom makes us peanut-butter-and-marshmallow sandwiches. Sometimes his Maltese, Toots, sits on my lap, while my cat, Zsa-Zsa, sits on his lap. We tickle their ears and sing dumb songs.

Today, all we can think or talk about is sixth grade. It's already late August and school is right around the corner. We're moving to Westcott Middle School from the elementary school down the street. That means that I'll be taking a bus to school every morning instead of walking with Jeff.

Mom got a letter from school the other day that listed the different sixth grade homerooms. I'm in 10A. Jeff is in 11B. I hate the fact that Jeff and I won't be in the same room. It will be the first time in all of our years in school together that we'll start each day in a different class with a different teacher. My best girlfriends, Leslie and Cristina, are in my homeroom, so I guess I'll survive.

But it won't be the same.

"Westcott has an awesome soccer team," Jeff mumbles, taking a final lick of his drippy Popsicle.

"Yeah, everyone knows that," I say.

Jeff likes soccer more than almost anything

else — even more than Toots. And that's saying something. He's been dreaming about winning a World Cup title since he was little. Fifth grade soccer camp, and fourth grade camp before that, just didn't cut the mustard. He has at least three pairs of cleats in his closet. Late this summer, Jeff was a part of this youth soccer league in our town. The kids told him that even though he was going into sixth grade, sometimes really good players were allowed to join the seventh and eighth grade middle school team. Now that's all he can talk about. He wants to be the exception to the rule.

"What are *you* going to do at Westcott?" Jeff asks with the usual daydream-y look in his eye that he always gets when thinking about soccer.

"What do you mean? Like after school?"

Jeff nods. "Yeah."

"I haven't really thought about it. I guess I'll try out for the school play, or maybe the school paper," I reply, licking my sticky, cherry fingers.

"Yeah," Jeff grunts. "You would."

"What is that supposed to mean?"

"*Nada.*"

I stand up and readjust my shorts, leaning back just a little so the sun isn't in my eyes. "Don't be a toad," I caution him, wagging my index finger in his face.

Jeff laughs and pinches me on the arm.

"Ribbit," he croaks, dancing off the porch steps.

Ow! I can almost feel the imaginary steam escaping out of my ears as I chase him around a tree, circle his shed, and speed back up the porch steps.

"Tag, you're it," I shout, leaning in for the touch. But just as I brush his arm, I catch my toe on a step and go flying.

Splat.

Jeff gets this stunned look for a split second. Then he bursts into a fit of hyena laughter. Here I am, sprawled on the steps, and he doesn't even try to help me up.

Instead, he *tags* me.

"You're it again!" Jeff hollers.

Just then, two boys appear at the fence gate near the side of Jeff's house. It's Jeff's best guy friends, Peter and Anthony. They're starting sixth grade at Westcott in a few weeks, too.

"Hey, Taryn, nice fall," Peter calls out to me.

I want to laugh, but my knee is killing me.

Jeff shoots me an abrupt look that says, "Okay, see you later. I have to hang out with the guys now." He's been giving me that look all summer long. We used to hang out together, the four of us, but lately they don't seem to want a girl around. I'm not sure why.

I wish I could pull off my own shoe and hit Jeff on the head with it, right there in front of his friends, so he would know how it feels. But somehow I don't think a flimsy pink flip-flop will have quite the same effect as his smelly sneaker. And I don't really want to hurt anyone, especially not him.

So I slink away from the boys, taking the hint, waving and hiking back through the break in Jeff's just-painted gray fence. In a few minutes, I'm back in my own yard, sidestepping my mother's purple daisies.

My brother Tim is lying in a lawn chair with his sunglasses on. He's as ginger-brown as an almond. He's spent the whole summer perfecting his tan. His girlfriend, Amy, works at a tanning parlor. The two of them look like an unnatural color to me, but I'm no tanning expert.

"Yo, Taryn, you got a phone call," Tim calls out to me.

"From who?" I ask.

"Dr. Wexler," Tim says, giving me a dramatic, low whistle and peering over the tops of his dark shades. "He wanted to schedule your eye exam. Man, are you in trouble, sis. That guy's Dr. Dread if you ask me."

"Ha, ha, ha . . . No one asked you," I groan, rolling my eyes and trying to act cool. I skip up the steps up to our house and push open the screen door.

The last person in the world I want to think about right now is Dr. Wexler.

Ever since I found out that my eyes don't work right, Tim's been trying to scare me about the optometrist. I hate to admit it, but his big-brother tactics are beginning to work. I'm trying hard not to be scared about the whole experience, but how am I supposed to feel about wearing glasses for the rest of my life? I know Tim's right about Dr. Wexler, too. Everyone says that guy has cold hands and death breath when he leans in to check your vision.

It all started at school last year, when I couldn't see the board. I didn't say anything at first, but then my grades started to slip. Then I found myself getting eye aches and sitting really close to the TV. And then I failed that stupid eye test the nurse gave me. The only reason I'm getting glasses at all is because Mom and Dad didn't give me a choice. Otherwise, I'd be perfectly content to walk around in a blurry haze for the rest of my life.

When I wander into the kitchen, I'm not surprised to find Mom there, chopping carrots.

"Are you in or out?" she asks me. "I'm trying a new recipe and I need all the taste buds I can find."

Mom's always experimenting in the kitchen. I think she dreams of being on Iron Chef one day, making weird dishes with rutabaga and octopus. I prefer grilled cheese myself.

"I'm in," I say, and take a seat at the table. My other brothers are, of course, nowhere to be found. "What's on the menu today, Mom?"

Her face lights up and she pushes some kind of salad in front of me. It smells like vinegar and onions. Cautiously, I lift a forkful into my mouth.

"So? So?" Mom hops up and down in front of me, looking for some kind of reaction.

Of course, I know what to say.

"Deeeee-licious," I mumble, choking down the salad. Mom beams.

Dad says Mom's sick of predictable dinners, so she's always looking for new recipes to try. And all summer I've been trying, really trying to deal. But it's hard.

And it's not just about the food.

School starts in exactly two weeks and I want to know one thing: Isn't there some way to make sure that, in sixth grade, things can just stay the way they've always been?